Leonardo Murphy

Russell F. Moran

Leonardo Murphy

Coddington Press

Copyright © 2019 by Russell F. Moran

Printed in the United States of America

ISBN-13: 978-0-578-21568-6

This book is a work of fiction. The characters, names, incidents, dialogue, and plot are the products of the author's imagination or are used fictitiously. Any resemblance to actual persons or events is purely coincidental.

Covers and text design by LuAnn T. Palazzo
Covers art by Leonardo da Vinci

www.morancom.com

DEDICATION

This book is dedicated to the inventors of the world.

ACKNOWLEDGEMENTS

As always, I thank my wife, Lynda, for her attentive reading, rereading, and editing of my many drafts, and for laughing at my jokes. I also thank my friend and editor, John White, for his keen editorial eye. And I especially thank my readers, many of whom are a constant source of inspiration and encouragement for me.

AUTHOR'S NOTE

You will find a Cast of Characters after the last chapter of the book. It can be frustrating to come across a character on page 150, who you first met on page 20, especially if you've put the book down for a few days. I've seen this done in Russian literature, and I happily add a cast of characters to *Leonardo Murphy* as well as my other novels.

Chapter 1

put a satellite into orbit without a rocket and I did it for under a thousand dollars, something all the experts thought was impossible. I used a balloon filled with helium attached to a small jet turbine engine that I bought used on eBay for $500. The satellite was small, only four inches in diameter, but it sported a high-powered camera, not exactly the Hubble, but it took great pictures. I bought the camera on Amazon for $250. The balloon carried the jet engine to the upper atmosphere, and then the engine fired the satellite into space.

Not bad for a 12-year-old kid.

So where do I get the money for something like that? Two years ago, my dad gave me $1,000 for my 10th birthday so that I could fund my increasingly expensive hobbies. He told me that I could only spend 10 percent of the fund each year. Therefore, in the first year I could only spend $100. Not good. So, I read two books on stock trading and then invested the $1,000. Dad opened the brokerage account for me. In just under two years the investment had grown to $1,650,000, more than enough to fund my hobbies along the way. I also bought my parents a brand-new Mercedes-Maybach for $195,000. My folks are neat people.

Mom and Dad insisted on calling me "Billy," even though I kept telling them that my name was Leonardo. I had nothing against the name William, or Billy, but I wanted to carry the name of my all-time favorite hero, Leonardo da Vinci, the most talented inventor of all time. Leonardo da Vinci is known as a polymath, a person of wide-ranging knowledge on a huge array of subjects. Some of the things he busied himself with included anatomy, architecture, astronomy, botany, cartography, engineering, geology, history, inventing, literature, mathematics, music, painting, science, sculpture, and writing. He is considered the father of paleontology, ichnology, and architecture. Also, most people think of him as one of the greatest painters of all time. In his spare time, he invented the helicopter and the army tank. People think of Leonardo da Vinci as the classic Renaissance man. I think of myself that way too.

So, no, my name's not Billy, it's Leonardo, which I think has a nice ring to it when you hook it up with Murphy.

To show my parents how serious I was, I hired a high-priced lawyer to get me a legal name change. The guy explained that he would do the paperwork, but that it wouldn't be official until I turned 18. That didn't stop him from charging me $5,000. I convinced my parents that my name is Leonardo. So what do they call me now? Leo, of course.

I must admit that I'm smart. My IQ clocks in at 295, just shy of the highest ever recorded. A genius is generally considered to be someone with an IQ around 145, so I easily fit into that category. The guy who scored the highest (300) was William James Sidis, born in 1898 and died in 1944 at the somewhat young age of 46. But my research showed me that Mr. Sidis' IQ test records were never found, so who knows, maybe I'm the smartest guy who ever lived. I should add that IQ tests didn't exist in the time of Leonardo da Vinci. Maybe he had a higher IQ than me, or maybe not. The man who holds the third highest IQ record, next to mine, is Christopher Michael Langan, born in 1952 with an IQ between

190 and 200. One interesting thing about Langan is that he believes in God, like I do, and once said, "You can prove the existence of God, the soul, and an afterlife, using mathematics." Cool.

But having a big brain doesn't mean anything unless you put it to use. When I was four years old I began to study languages. By the time I was five, I was fluent in Chinese Mandarin, French, German, Italian, Japanese, Spanish, and Russian.

As a 12-year-old genius I had all the potential to be an insufferable, obnoxious brat, but I'm not, or at least I don't think I am. My parents tell me they admire my humility. I guess they do, otherwise they wouldn't say so.

The reason I'm not obnoxious is because of my late great-grandfather, Ezekiel Murphy, who passed away four years ago when I was eight years old. I'm not the only Murphy with an odd first name. Like me, Grandpa Ezekiel insisted on being called by his full name, never "Zeke." Grandpa Ezekiel was my second favorite human being, right after Leonardo da Vinci. He died at the age of 98 while in the hospital with a heart problem. I visited him every day. Like me, he was smart, and held 300 patents, awarded the most recent one when he was 96. I'll never forget the day he died. I was alone with him in his hospital room, my parents due to come later. The reason I'll never forget the day he died, besides my sadness, were the words he said to me.

"Leonardo," he said, (I didn't have to convince him that my name was Leonardo) "you're a bright boy, one of the brightest in the world, if not *the* brightest. There's not much I can tell you, because you're amazing at figuring out things for yourself, but make me a promise, and never forget it—Whatever you do, don't be an asshole."

Chapter 2

"Don't be an asshole." It's been four years since Grandpa Ezekiel died, and his words still ring true to me. One of the reasons the words are still with me is that Grandpa Ezekiel never cussed—ever. His idea of a four-letter word was heck or darn. That's why he shocked me when he said the word asshole. He was brilliant at making somebody understand what he wanted to say, and one cussword did the trick.

I think I'm doing a pretty good job of heeding his words. I could easily become the obnoxious jerk he warned me about, especially when I notice the bozos around me.

Jimmy Munson is a case in point. In my freshman year at Northside High School I was nine years old and looked it. I had been accelerated into senior high school, or at least my brain was. My body was still that of a little kid. Jimmy Munson, age 14 at the time, was also a freshman. He decided to dedicate his young life to bullying me, not just mentally but physically. One day, as I was closing the door to my locker, he hauled back and punched me in the nose. After crying like the nine-year-old that I was, I decided to do what I always do when I have a problem—I hit the books and did research. I studied self-defense.

After reading up on every martial art there was, I decided that I would take lessons in judo, which means "the gentle way." I realized that was definitely for me. I'm not too crazy about violence. In fact it makes me sick. I didn't want to study something like karate, with all sorts of punching and kicking. My parents thought it was a great idea, and Dad went with me to the local training school known as a *dojo*. Dad was good friends with the owner, a nice guy named Ben. I threw myself into my judo training like I do with all my projects. When I concentrate on something, I always get results—fast. There are two broad grades or rankings in judo; the beginning grades known as *kyu*, and the more advanced levels known as *dan*. Because I read and speak fluent Japanese I had no trouble learning the terminology. But, of course, you don't learn judo by speaking Japanese. You need to train and practice, practice, practice. I did just that. Within two months I had achieved the *dan* grade, the first level of a black belt. Ben, the owner of the dojo, was amazed at how fast I progressed. My dad, a senior FBI official, is in terrific physical shape and knows how to defend himself. He often challenged me to a judo match. I let him win about half the time—hey, he's my dad.

One day I stopped at my locker on my way to the next class. Jimmy Munson liked to hang around the lockers because it was easy to select a target to bully. I wasn't his only target, but I was his favorite. I reached up to retrieve a book from the top shelf when I felt a sharp pain in my back. It was Jimmy Munson practicing his punches. I was angry, of course, but I noticed something besides the anger—I wasn't afraid. I thought I'd lose my temper, but I took a deep breath instead. Only assholes lose their temper. Jimmy raised his right fist and drew back, apparently aiming his next punch at my face. I stepped back and grabbed his arm as he swung at me. I turned, still holding his arm and flipped him over my side. As he landed, he slammed his head into the locker door. He shouted a string of cusswords as he stood up, raising his fist for another attempt. I flipped him in the other direction, being careful not to let his head strike the lockers again. I really didn't want to hurt the guy, I thought, amazed that I had such a thought. The discipline I learned in judo came to my aid—and to Jimmy's. He started to get up again. From the angle between him and me, I could have broken his jaw, but I didn't. Another swing, another body flip. He landed face down. I grabbed his right arm and locked it behind his back. I didn't want to be late for class, so I figured it was time to end this nonsense.

"Jimmy," I said, "I've heard that you're flunking math. I'll be happy to help you after school, but first I want you to promise you'll stop attacking me. Deal?"

"Fuck off, shithead," Jimmy replied.

"In that case," I said, "thank you for the workout."

That was three years ago. I'm now a 12-year-old senior, and Jimmy Munson is 17. He hasn't attacked me since. As expected, Jimmy flunked math. Unfortunately, he was still an asshole.

But one day, something amazing happened. At my graduation, Jimmy walked up to me and reached out for a handshake. He wasn't graduating that day because he needed to go to summer school to take his chemistry class over. So, what's he doing at graduation? I wondered. "Leonardo, I owe you an apology."

"For what?" I said. I couldn't believe what I'd just heard.

"For bullying you a few years ago. I'm sorry. That's all I can say."

"Well thank you, Jimmy, that means a lot to me. Why the big change, if I may ask?"

"I found something I'd been ignoring too long. I found God. I've been going to church regularly, and I found that I believe in God. I decided to pattern my life after Him, and I realized that he wouldn't act like I did a few years ago. So, again, please accept my apology. You're one heck of a guy, and I just needed to say that."

"Jimmy, my offer is still open. I know you'll be going to summer school for chemistry. I'll be happy to help you."

"Leonardo, I appreciate that. I accept your offer."

So that summer I showed Jimmy the secrets of the periodic table of elements, and he showed me the way to God. I would always go to church with my parents, but never considered myself religious. Jimmy changed that. He'd often go with me and my parents to Mass at St. Mark's Episcopal Church. Jimmy and I are now good friends. With my help, he finished first in his chemistry class.

In a way, grandpa's telling me not to be an asshole was really a religious message. If you're an asshole, you're not following the word of God. Jimmy seems to have gotten that message.

Chapter 3

'm lucky to have the greatest parents in the world. They sometimes scratch their heads, wondering how their small but big-brained son got to be that way. I love academic stuff, studying, researching, writing, and just plain thinking. Heck, I was just accepted to Harvard University at age 12.

My folks have active occupations. Yes, their jobs require brains, but also a lot of physical action. Mom is the chief detective of the NYPD homicide unit. Mom's a pretty lady, soft spoken and slender. She wears her hair short because she never knows when she's going to have to run somewhere and doesn't want to fuss with it. She wears a Glock pistol on her waist, but she still manages to look feminine. She also has a great sense of humor. Whenever I correct her for calling me Leo instead of Leonardo, she always insists that I call her "Mother Dearest," rather than Mom. "If I have to use four syllables when talking to you," Mom said, "I think your mother deserves the same." Mom is way cool, I mean Mother Dearest.

Dad is no desk jockey either. He's the head of the FBI Joint Terrorism Task Force. He, too, carries a pistol, and sometimes an M16 semi-automatic rifle. You would think that when they talk shop over dinner, it would sound like a *Criminal Minds* rerun. But it isn't that way. Sure, some of their work shows up in conversation, but it's not a lot of bragging nonsense. They're real pros, and they know how to leave the mayhem of their jobs behind them. I think it's totally excellent that they don't tell me to leave the room when they talk about the world's latest chaos. They seem to know that my mind can process information in a way that's beyond my actual age. I also help them analyze their cases.

I saw Mom interviewed on TV last week by a reporter from NBC. The segment was about a big multiple-murder case that Mom was handling. A total of 12 bodies. Yuck. The reporter was a bit of a jerk, well not a bit of a jerk, a complete jerk. He kept asking Mom why no arrests had been made yet. I mean, hey, the murders occurred the day before the show aired. I think the reporter was trying to show the viewers that he's a "hard-hitting journalist." Yeah, right. Mom, in her calm way, simply smiled and answered the guy's questions without getting angry. I think she should have collared the guy for being an asshole, but I guess that's not really against the law. It should be.

And just the other day, Dad was on TV being interviewed by the same "hard-hitting journalist" who questioned Mom. Dad was working on a huge terrorism case that involved dozens of possible terrorists, not to mention a few bombings that had already occurred. The guy wanted names—yeah, the names of terror suspects. Dad is as cool as mom, but sometimes he loses it—slightly. Dad just looked at the guy as if he was a squirrel singing rock and roll and cracked up laughing right in front of the camera. I'm proud of Mom and Dad. They're tough law enforcement people, but they don's see their jobs as just busting heads. They think, they analyze, and they solve a lot of cases—with my help.

Speaking of television, I don't watch it much because I have other things to do. Television is passive, and I like my brain to be active. But tomorrow I'm going to be interviewed by the most beautiful woman in the world. I will be a guest on *The Ellen Bellamy Show*, the most popular show on daytime TV. Mom suggested that I get a haircut first, and I agreed. I'm going to ask the barber to put some of that nice-smelling hair-gook stuff on my head, just to show Ellen Bellamy that I care.

Chapter 4

ood afternoon ladies and gentlemen, and welcome to CBS and *The Ellen Bellamy Show*. I'm your host—you guessed it—Ellen Bellamy."

"We have a special guest today, a young man who intimidates me. As many of you know I graduated from MIT with degrees in engineering and architecture and then I got an MBA from Wharton. But after talking to our guest I feel like a complete dummy. Leonardo Murphy is a freshman at Harvard University at the young age of 12, having finished high school in two years. To say that Leonardo is bright is to give new meaning to the word *understatement*. He has the second highest IQ ever recorded and comes up with answers before people even finish the question. He was born William Murphy but changed his name in honor of the man he admires most, Leonardo da Vinci, a man who just may have been as smart as young Mr. Murphy."

Ellen Bellamy is a really nice lady, as you would expect from someone with the most popular show on daytime TV. She's also gorgeous. Her husband Rick is the Secretary of Homeland Security and a good friend of my father, a senior FBI agent. The Bellamys invited me to have dinner with them tonight after Ellen's show, and I can't wait. But first I needed to sit through Ellen's embarrassing questions. I get a lot of interview requests, most of which I ignore. But when I was invited to be a guest on her show I jumped at the chance. Although I seldom watch TV, I once tuned into her show because she was interviewing a professor of physics at Harvard, a man whose course I will be taking next semester. I was impressed with her brains, not to mention her looks.

"So, tell us, Leonardo, how does it feel to be enrolled at one of the best universities in the world at the tender age of 12?"

"Harvard's great, but most of the students are a lot taller than me. They're all pretty smart, which I like. I think it's good to be challenged, and also good to be around intelligent people, people like you."

She smiled and winked at me, and I winked back. When you're 12 years old you can flirt with an adult woman and get away with it because grownups think it's cute. Six months ago, I got my first hard-on. I hope she doesn't ask me to stand up. *That* wouldn't be cute.

"From what I've heard about you, Leonardo, besides having a brilliant mind, you're also known as a gentleman. Do you owe that to your parents? My husband and I know them both and I think they're terrific people."

"I consider myself lucky to have great parents. I don't know if I'm the gentleman you say I am, but in answer to your question, I got my politeness from my late great grandfather, Ezekiel Murphy. I think I got my brains from him too. Shortly before he died he gave me the greatest advice I've ever been given. 'Whatever you do, Leonardo, don't be an as…jerk,' he told me.' For some reason those words have stuck with me."

"Leonardo, I understand that you launched a satellite into orbit without a rocket for under a thousand dollars. If I hadn't verified that information I would have said it's impossible, but you did it. You accomplished something that the experts said couldn't be done. At the age of 12 you've made scientific history. Can you tell us how you came up with the idea?"

"Well, Ellen, it isn't rocket science." I can't believe I cracked such a dumb joke, but from the laughter it was obvious that Ellen and the audience enjoyed it.

"I just put together two facts. I knew that a helium balloon can reach a high altitude. I combined that with the idea of using a jet turbine engine rather than a rocket, because the balloon would take the engine near the edge of space, giving it a running start. You can accomplish the same thing by firing a rocket from a high-flying jet aircraft, but my method is a lot cheaper and more efficient. I had a lot of fun with that project, but unfortunately, because the satellite is in such a low orbit, it will burn up in a few months as it reenters the earth's atmosphere."

"I've heard that you love to work on projects, Leonardo. Do you have anything on your plate now that you would like to tell us about? I read that you enjoy working with artificial intelligence. There's nothing artificial about *your* intelligence, but let's hear what you're up to."

"Yes, Ellen, artificial intelligence is something that fascinates me. I think it's the future of technology. I've come up with an algorithm that enables a computer to write a novel. This project really took off after I enrolled at Harvard. The computer lab has the computational power that I didn't have at home. I'm still tweaking the program, but I expect that Austen will soon begin the first chapter. She's already completed an outline."

"Austen?"

"Yes, I named the program after Jane Austen, one of my favorite novelists."

"But Leonardo, something confuses me. Computers can't think. They just perform tasks that we program into them. How can a computer write a novel, something that requires a lot of thinking?"

"The answer is data—a lot of data, a ton of data. Because of the massive storage space on the computers at Harvard, I was able to pour in millions of words, real words from real books. The first task that I assigned Austen was to read novels, 10 of them. That process took three months because I had to do a lot of tweaking to make sure she was getting it. Austen now knows the basic structure of a novel. Next, I'll turn her loose, so to speak, on the millions of words I uploaded into the mainframe's memory. So far, she's written a few paragraphs as a test. Here's the opening paragraph of a book she's working on:

"I looked into his eyes, trying to understand what he meant when he said, 'Don't go near the water. Alligators bite.' I didn't know what he meant because we were about 10 miles from the nearest body of water. Every time I asked for an explanation, he just kept saying 'alligators bite.' After about 15 minutes of the ridiculous conversation, I had my answer. The man was totally insane. This could turn out to be a problem, a big problem. He had the car keys, or at least I thought he did. He said that an alligator ate them. So, there I was in a house in a remote part of the county with a crazy person who insisted that an alligator ate the car keys."

"So, what do you think, Ellen? Does that sound like a book you'd like to read?"

The audience broke out into applause. I guess they'd like to read the book.

"Honestly Leonardo, it sounds like the beginning of a thrilling story. From what I know about writing fiction, you've obeyed one of the first rules for a novelist—make the reader want to turn the page. I would really like to know if the alligator ate the car keys. When the book is finished, can I buy a signed copy?"

"The book cover will show a collaboration between two authors, Austen and me. So, you'll get my signature. I won't be the only author, of course, but let's face it, Austen can't do it without my programming. I'm working on a cursive writing module for Austen, so by the time the book is finished you may be able to get a book signed by both authors."

"Speaking of books, Leonardo, I understand that Yale University Press has recently published a nonfiction book that you wrote. Please tell us about it."

"It's a book titled *Differential Calculus for Busy Students*. I know it's kind of a wise-guy title, but I figured a bit of humor may help it to sell. It's 630 pages long, so I tried to keep it light."

"So, you're a 12-year-old young man, and you've written a huge book on a complex mathematical subject. How long did it take you to write it?"

"It took me six months, and then it took another six months to go through editing at my publisher. I tried to tell them that all the facts and formulas were correct, but they wanted to edit the book anyway. The editor didn't change one word or formula. The reason it me took so long to write it is that I was busy with other projects like Austen, not to mention my course load."

"I hope it's okay if I ask this question, but how is the book selling?"

"It's required reading at 85 university math programs as of yesterday."

"Can you tell us about some of your other projects?"

"I'm working on a labor-saving drone that paints the stripes on football fields. That may not sound like a big deal, but a friend of my parents is a pro-football referee, and he convinced the NFL to give me a $2 million contract. After that project I'm going to start research on more artificial intelligence machines. I believe that's the future, and a lot of it is showing up now, such as my Austen program."

"Leo..."

"Leonardo."

"Sorry, Leonardo. It's been a pleasure having you on my show, and I hope to have you back soon. You're a fascinating young man."

"And you're a very nice lady, Ellen." She's also drop-dead gorgeous, but I didn't say that, of course. Oh, my goodness, I have to stand up now.

Chapter 5

I thought it was really cool being a guest on the famous *Ellen Bellamy Show*. Because my folks are good friends with Ellen and her husband, Rick, they said it would be okay if I stayed at the Bellamys' apartment for a couple of days while they were away. It was a Friday and I didn't have classes at Harvard until Monday. Two full days of staring at the beautiful Ellen Bellamy. *Don't be an asshole*, I reminded myself.

After Ellen's show was over at 4 p.m., we went downtown in a limousine to the Bellamys' apartment. Rick Bellamy was working from his New York office at 26 Federal Plaza, just a few blocks from their condo. Mr. Bellamy is the Secretary of Homeland Security. My dad is the head of the FBI Joint Terrorism Task Force, so he and Rick Bellamy see each other a lot. Dad's office is right down the hall from his. Mr. Bellamy got home a few minutes after us. As soon as he walked in the door, he and Ellen hugged and kissed. Lucky guy.

Wow, I'd never seen such a big apartment. The place covers two floors of a building in the Greenwich Village section of Manhattan. I had a suite all to myself, including a ginormous bathroom. My folks told me that *The Ellen Bellamy Show* is even more popular than *Judge Judy*, which airs on CBS right after Ellen's show. I read that Judge Judy makes over $45 million a year, so I can see how the Bellamys can afford such a big apartment.

"So, this is the young man Jack Murphy told me so much about," Mr. Bellamy said. "I saw you on Ellen's show this afternoon. I gotta tell you, Leo, you impressed me, and I'm not easily impressed."

"Leonardo."

"Of course, Leonardo."

"Your parents are proud of you, which doesn't surprise me after listening to you on Ellen's show. You have an enormous amount of knowledge on an enormous range of subjects. My God, you're only 12 years old and you're studying at Harvard."

Mr. Bellamy was extremely polite and friendly. It was easy to like this guy.

When we sat down at the huge table in the huge dining room, I wondered where the food would come from. I was hungry as a dog, and I was glad we would have an early dinner at 5:30 p.m. My stomach was a little nervous before going on the air—the show was live, not taped, and I skipped lunch. The maid, Alexis, came in with our plates. A maid? I was not used to that kind of luxury. The Bellamys, being really nice people, treated Alexis like a good friend, not a maid. The food was excellent. We had roast chicken with wild rice and string beans, nothing fancy, but delicious.

I was happy the Bellamys treated me like an adult. I was worried that the evening would be all about, "So how's our cute little genius friend doing?" They both insisted that I call them by their first names. I felt a bit uncomfortable at first—Hey, I'm a 12-year-old—but soon it felt natural.

"You look like you've sprouted some more gray hairs since this morning, honey," Ellen said to Rick. "Let me guess, more of that MS-13 crap." They brought me into their conversation like I was family. Cool.

"Yeah, as usual," Mr. Bellamy said. "In the past five days there have been 20 horrible murders just in the New York Metropolitan area. Familiar stuff. All the murders were done with machetes, preceded by lengthy torture. And we've yet to make an arrest."

"I'm sorry, Leonardo," Ellen said. "I hope we're not upsetting your stomach with talk like this after a nice dinner."

"It isn't a problem, Ellen," I said. "I'm quite familiar with the MS-13 gang. I just finished a 125-page research paper on that subject for my political science class. I showed it to my dad before handing it in. Although Dad seldom orders me around, he insisted that I shouldn't hand in the paper. He said that if any of the MS-13 thugs heard that I wrote about the gang, I'd be marked for death."

"Your father told me he had something interesting to show me," Rick said, "something that you wrote. I guess the MS-13 paper is it."

"I just gave it to him yesterday, and he said he'd give it to you after he read it. I needed to do another paper in a hurry to meet my professor's deadline. So, I wrote a paper comparing New York City transit fares to gasoline consumption over the past 25 years. It took me almost six hours."

"Your dad was right to convince you not to hand in the paper," Rick said. "As I'm sure you know, that gang is populated by the most ruthless and cruel people we've ever seen. Ellen's producers have been going crazy trying to book an MS-13 expert on her show. I warned them that they could be endangering the life of the expert, not to mention Ellen's."

"Yes, Dad convinced me, and after what you just said, I think he was right. I'd be putting a target on my back. May I make a suggestion?"

"Sure, what is it?"

"I recommend to you, as I recommended to my dad, that you use my paper as a training manual for any agent involved with MS-13. My research showed me that a lot of incorrect information is floating around about this gang, information that could lead law enforcement in the wrong direction. I don't believe in false modesty, so let me just say that my paper is the most accurate document concerning MS-13 that you will find—anywhere."

Mr. Bellamy just stared at me wide-eyed. He didn't comment, just nodded. I think I got his attention.

"Rick, I never asked you, but how did the gang get its name?" Ellen said, breaking the awkward silence.

"I bet Leonardo can tell us."

"MS stands for *Mara Salvatrucha*," I said. "Some people think the gang is named for *La Mara*, a street gang in San Salvador, and the Salvatrucha guerrillas who fought in the Salvadoran Civil War. Also, the word *mara* means gang in Central American slang and is derived from *marabunta*, an aggressive type of ant. "Salvatrucha" may be a combination of the words *Salvadoran* and *trucha*, a Central American dialect word for being alert. The number 13, most agree, is for the letter "m" being the 13th letter in the alphabet. So, the marketing department of the gang likes the brand, MS-13."

"Marketing department?" Ellen said, laughing. "And how many members are in this lovely club?"

"Estimates vary, but I think Rick will agree that the number is somewhere between eight and ten thousand in the US, and thirty to fifty thousand worldwide."

We moved from the dining room table to the den. Ellen kicked off her shoes, stretched her beautiful legs, and perched her pretty feet on an ottoman. Oh, my goodness, I thought. I hope nobody asks me to stand up.

"I can hear the gears in your brain clicking, Rick," Ellen said. "A penny for your thoughts."

"I want to check with my legal department, but I wonder if there's a problem hiring a 12-year-old as a consultant. What do you think, Leonardo? Do you think you could fit the FBI and Homeland Security into your busy schedule? You have knowledge that we badly need. You wouldn't need to leave Harvard. We can consult by secure phone and our Intranet."

"Are you serious, Mr. Secretary, I mean Rick?"

"Yes, I am. I want to discuss this with your parents first, of course, but I'm sure they would be proud to have you serve your country in such an important way. MS-13 is the most evil organization on the planet. If we can harvest your brilliant mind, you can help us defeat these creeps. And we'll pay you good money."

"If my folks say it's okay, I'll be happy to do it. If I can help put an end to that horrible gang, I'll consider it an honor."

On Sunday afternoon I wrapped up my stay with the Bellamys and headed back to Boston. As soon as I get to my room I'm going to set my DVR to record *The Ellen Bellamy Show* at 3 p.m. every weekday. I don't watch much television, but I wouldn't dream of missing Ellen's show. I guess adults would think of my feelings for Ellen as "a crush." Truth is, I felt like I was madly in love with her. She's a foot taller than me and 18 years older (I checked her out on Wikipedia). Oh, right—*Don't be an asshole.*

Chapter 6

"Secretary Bellamy on line one for you, Jack," Agent Murphy's assistant said.

"Hi Rick. I hope you enjoyed having Leonardo for the weekend."

"Totally enjoyed it, Jack. Your son is not only brilliant, he's a complete gentleman. There's something I want to talk to you about. I can come to your office now, if that's okay with you."

Bellamy walked down the hall to Jack Murphy's office.

"That kid of yours is amazing, Jack. The paper he wrote that you left in my in-box this morning nailed it for me. I read every word of it and I'm blown away by his scholarly approach. I've heard about him, read about him, and watched him recently on Ellen's show. We were happy to host him for a weekend. He is an absolute genius, and a damn nice guy to boot. I couldn't believe that we were hosting a kid. I mean he looks like a kid and has the voice of one, but Ellen and I both realized we were talking to an adult, a somewhat young one, but definitely an adult. I don't know if he told you, but I want to hire him as a consultant to both the FBI and Homeland Security on the MS-13 problem. Safe to say that nobody on earth has studied that gang like Leonardo, and I'd love to turn his brain loose on helping us put an end to those bastards. I told him that I would talk to you about it first."

"I have to agree with you, Rick, but, speaking as his father, I want his identity kept secret. You know how MS-13 operates, and I don't want them operating on my son."

"I totally agree, Jack. To keep a tight lid on this operation, I want only you or me to speak to him. He'll need a top-secret clearance, of course, but I'll go right to the White House if I need to. President Morton listens to me. We'll pay him on the same scale we pay any other top-level consultant. I hope it won't interfere with his studies."

"Interfere with his studies? Leonardo gives new meaning to the phrase 'multi-tasking.' He can solve the quadratic equation—in his head—while playing Bach on the piano and singing words to a song he just composed. In his first semester at Harvard he designed an artificial intelligence program that can write novels and then he wrote a book on differential calculus. He still pulled a straight-A average. I think you have a great idea, Rick. In the short time it took him to write that paper he learned more about MS-13 than anybody in the world. I'm glad he spent the weekend with you folks."

"Oh, another thing," Bellamy said, laughing, "I think he's in love with Ellen."

Chapter 7

eonardo, it's Dad. I remembered that you don't have classes on Friday. I want you to meet me at my office. Somebody else will be there too."

"Oh, you must mean…"

"Leonardo please say no more. My line is secure, but I don't know about yours."

As a big-time FBI executive, Dad is always concerned about security.

"I'll check the train schedule, Dad. What time do you want to meet me?"

"Forget the train schedule. I'll have a car pick you up outside your dorm at 8 a.m. Friday."

Wow. How cool is this? I'm sure they want to see me about that consulting job Rick Bellamy talked about. A car with my own driver? Neat. I'm sure the other guy at the meeting will be Rick Bellamy. Maybe he'll bring Ellen along. When I close my eyes, I can still remember the scent of her perfume. I should really stop thinking like this, but what can I do? Actually, I know what I can do: *Don't be an asshole.*

My car—*my car,* pulled up to the rear entrance of 26 Federal Plaza. I had been there a few times before to visit Dad, but this is the first time somebody held the door for me. Cool. After I went through the metal detector a guy escorted me to Dad's office. I was not feeling like your average 12-year-old.

"Hi, Leonardo. We're going to meet in Secretary Bellamy's office down the hall."

We walked into Rick's office and he was there along with a woman who looked familiar. I guessed she was about 60 years old, judging from her slightly gray hair. She was pleasant looking, and wore an expensive no-nonsense business suit. I thought I'd seen her on TV.

"Leonardo," Bellamy said. "so good to see you again. Let me introduce Sarah Watson, Director of the FBI, who's visiting us today here in New York. Sarah will do the honors."

The honors? I thought. Am I being decorated with some kind of medal?

"Sarah will now swear you in as a deputy agent of the Federal Bureau of Investigation. Your top-secret clearance has been approved, and the action Sarah is about to take has been cleared through the Senate Intelligence Committee. Because you're a minor, your dad here will give his consent as your parent."

Wow. I allowed myself the pleasant feeling of being hot stuff. I only wished Ellen Bellamy could be there. *Okay, stop.*

Chapter 8

Government people love to have meetings. I've always heard that. I once wrote a paper on synchronous versus asynchronous communication. With asynchronous communication, where you don't need to have a give and take, most stuff can be handled by email or text, such as "Be in my office at 10." But, "*Can* you be in my office at 10?" requires synchronous communication and can be handled a lot faster by phone. But government types, being government types, love the synchronicity of a meeting. Sometimes meetings are necessary, such as the one that was about to start. After Director Watson swore me in, I figured we'd go have lunch, but no, they wanted to have a meeting. It was just Sarah Watson, Rick Bellamy, my dad, and me.

"Sarah, you've been as close to this case as Jack or me, so why don't you bring Leonardo up to speed."

"I'd be happy to bring this young man up to speed," Watson said, "but truth is, he's the one who will bring us up to speed. Leonardo, I've heard and read so much about you that I feel like I know you. It's a pleasure and honor to meet you. Secretary Bellamy's idea of hiring you as a consultant was brilliant, if you ask me. He and your dad shared with me the MS-13 paper you wrote and I was flabbergasted. I thought I knew a lot about that pack of rats, but your paper amazed me with your scholarly research and analysis. So, tell us, since Rick floated the idea of hiring you, have you come up with any new thoughts?"

"Yes, Madam Director..."

"Hey, Leonardo, we consider you a colleague. Please call us by our first names, except your dad of course."

"Well, Sarah, in the past two days I've designed a computer algorithm that I think we'll find most helpful."

"You designed a computer algorithm involving MS-13 in two friggin days?"

"Yes, Sarah. Let me explain. As we all know, the ethnic makeup of MS-13 is mainly from El Salvador, Honduras, and Guatemala. But my research told me that the most common language for MS-13, in both correspondence and the spoken word, is Caliche, a slang dialect previously spoken only in El Salvador. That has changed and is still changing. I believe they prefer to communicate in Caliche because it's hard to understand, and few people in the world speak it. Caliche is based on a language called Nahuatl, which originated with indigenous people in Central America before the Spanish arrived. Even Google Translate, which is highly sophisticated software, gets tripped up with Caliche."

"Are you familiar with this language, Leonardo?"

"Yes, Dad. I understand it and speak it fluently."

They all cracked up.

"So, I did search after search. Because it came from a primitive language, there are a lot of spelling variations, but all told, I found 300 key words, including the different spellings. During my research, I hacked into a lot of websites that MS-13 uses—yes, I know how to hack computers and websites—and what I found shocked me. I've come to a conclusion."

"Well don't be shy," Rick Bellamy said. "What's your conclusion?"

"MS-13 leadership uses Caliche as a code—and I've broken the code."

Chapter 9

Good afternoon, ladies and gentlemen, Wolf Blitzer reporting for *CNN*. I have some amazing information about the notorious gang known as MS-13. *CNN* has just been told that no fewer than 3,000 gang members have been arrested in the United States, people who were wanted for almost every type of violent crime imaginable, including murder, rape, torture, and terrorism. MS-13 is known for unspeakable cruelty and violence. Initiation into the gang includes such things as a 'beat in,' where a potential new member is severely beaten before being granted entry into the ranks. The FBI estimates that there are between 8,000 and 10,000 MS-13 gang members in the United States, so an arrest of 3,000 is a huge percentage of the gang's membership. We asked if there is any reason for the sudden arrests and were told by FBI officials that they've gotten more sophisticated in the use of a computer database of gang members. There is a rumor, and I stress that it's an unconfirmed rumor, that a 12-year-old boy designed a computer algorithm to help law enforcement keep track of the violent gang. We have on the line FBI Director Sarah Watson."

"Hello, Wolf."

"Madam Director, what can you tell us about this good news?"

"It's a breakthrough, Wolf. As you know MS-13 is the epitome of evil and wanton violence. Not only have we arrested a large number of suspects, but many of them hold leadership positions in the gang."

"Director Watson, can you tell us anything about the rumor that a 12-year-old boy designed the software that helped nab these people?"

"Rumors are just that, Wolf, and that particular rumor is ridiculous," Watson lied. "As you know, the FBI, combined with the Department of Homeland Security, boasts a highly trained IT staff who collaborate on computer databases all the time. And they're adults, not children."

"There you have it, folks. Some truly good news about the most violent gang in existence. Let's hope that this is the beginning of the end of that hateful group."

"Who the hell leaked that information about a 12-year-old boy designing the MS-13 algorithm?" Jack Murphy shouted at a staff meeting. "I don't like the idea of my son in the crosshairs."

"I share Jack's anger about this," Sarah Watson said. "One of the hallmarks of MS-13 is revenge and retribution. Whoever leaked this information has put Jack's son's life in danger. I consider this offense so serious, I've asked the attorney general to appoint a special prosecutor to find the leaker. We may have to put young Leonardo into the Witness Protection Program."

Chapter 10

ongratulations, Eduardo. You are now our leader in New York," Angel Guevara said to Eduardo Lopez, the suddenly elevated MS-13 gang leader. Guevara is his assistant.

"You say congratulations, Angel, but we have a problem, a big fucking problem. Three thousand of our people have been rounded up, and we don't know how it happened. It will take me months to get things organized, and that's just here in New York. The first thing I need to do is get the drugs flowing again, our main source of money. Tell me, Angel, what do you know about this FBI attack on our organization?"

"We have insiders at the FBI as you know, Eduardo, but most of our information comes from the news. We heard about a new computer program that helps them track us, but we don't know any of the details, not that I'd understand them anyway."

"What about the stories I've been hearing about a 12-year-old kid designing the program?"

"I've spoken to Sancho Almeda, the dude in charge of spying on the feds for us. I tell you, Eduardo, Sancho is one smart guy. He put two and two together, and he thinks the story about the 12-year-old may be true. Ever hear about that kid, Leonardo Murphy?"

"Yeah, he's that little genius that everybody's been talking about. He was on television not long ago. Ellen Bellamy, that hot fox, interviewed him about his inventions and shit. He's only 12 years old but he's in college, Harvard I think. So, Sancho thinks this smart gringo kid may be working for the feds?"

"Guess what the little dude's father does for a living. He's an FBI agent, the fucking head of the Joint Terrorism Task Force, one of the groups that's been after us lately."

"Holy fucking shit. I think Sancho may be on to something. I think we should track that kid down and have one of little our 'talks' with him."

"Whoa, Eduardo. I have nothing against kicking the shit out of a wiseass little gringo, but if we touch a hair on his head, the feds will call out the fucking Marines on us. Remember, his old man is big-time FBI."

"Yeah, but I want to know exactly where this little genius is and what he's up to. We need to find a friendly Latino who works at Harvard and give him a lot of money. If we find that this Leonardo kid is fucking with us, we take him out. We can make it look like an accident. Sancho is good at shit like that."

Chapter 11

Jack Murphy, Sarah Watson, and Rick Bellamy met at Bellamy's office at 26 Federal Plaza. "We've got a gigantic problem and we need to act—fast," Bellamy said. "Hiring Jack's son as a consultant was my idea and that's why I'm taking personal responsibility for this. I'd like to find that son of a bitch who leaked the story and personally strip him of his pension. Jack, please repeat for Sarah what you've told me."

"As you two know, my wife, Rebecca, is chief detective of the NYPD homicide unit. Sometimes she's so perceptive, I think she should have *my* job. So, Rebecca and I were talking about this 12-year-old-boy leak, and what it could mean for Leonardo. Let's add up a few simple facts. First, my son is pretty famous, especially since he appeared on your wife's TV show, Rick. Everybody knows about the 'boy genius.' They also know that Leonardo is 12 years old, and that his old man is a senior FBI official. Now, if you're an MS-13 leader, wouldn't you figure that the designer of the computer program is none other than my son? And then what would you do about it? I don't even want to *think* about that."

"Your thoughts, Sarah?" Bellamy said.

"I think we all know what we have to do. Young Leonardo's life is in danger, it's that simple. We've got to get Leonardo into the Witness Protection Program—immediately. He'll have to take a leave of absence from Harvard. Hell, Harvard will take him back in a wink of an eye when he reapplies."

"Jack, I suggest you go to Boston immediately. Take a helicopter to Kennedy and one of our jets will fly you to Boston. I'll alert our local office to have a car waiting for you at Logan Airport. Meanwhile I'll talk to the head of the WPP and let him know he's about to host a young guest. MS-13 likes to move fast. We need to move faster."

Chapter 12

sat in my dorm room working on the latest tweaks to Austen, my novel writing program. I think the story is getting really interesting. My agent says the publisher, Random House, loves the concept—an alligator that ate the car keys. It was 2:30 p.m. and my favorite TV show, The Ellen Bellamy Show, will be on at three. Some of my classmates have dubbed my room *The Ellen Bellamy Room* because I hung so many pictures of her on the walls. Oh, my goodness, she's beautiful. If Grandpa Ezekiel is looking down on me from heaven, I think he's shaking his head. *Leonardo the asshole, reporting for duty.*

Looks like my MS-13 algorithm did the trick. Wow, they rounded up 3,000 of the creeps. My software enabled them to do what they've been trying to pull off for 10 years. I must admit, I felt proud, especially because I helped my dad do his job.

Okay, stop everything. Ellen's on the air.

It was a great show, as usual. I don't know what it was about, because I spent the entire hour staring at Ellen. She wore a pretty green dress and her hair was done up in a new style. Then my cell phone rang.

"Leonardo, it's Dad. I'm outside your dorm. We need to talk."

My God, I thought. This must be something big. A man as important as my dad wouldn't come all the way to Boston just to have a chat. But he's obsessive about security and that's probably why he didn't call me first to let me know he was coming.

Dad walked in and cracked up. "You have an interesting sense of decorating, Leonardo," he said as he looked at all the photos of Ellen Bellamy.

He pulled up a chair and sat facing me.

"I've said it a million times, and I'll say it again. Your MS-13 algorithm has put law enforcement ahead by years. Absolutely brilliant work, Leonardo, what I've come to expect of you."

Dad has a great way of making me feel good. But I'm sure he didn't come all the way to Boston just to flatter me.

"I'm sure you've heard the news reports that our program designer may have been a 12-year-old boy."

"Yeah, I thought it was pretty stupid for someone to leak that information."

"It's beyond stupid, it's criminal negligence. Sarah Watson has arranged for a special prosecutor to find the leaker. Your mom and I, along with Sarah Watson and Rick Bellamy, have come to a conclusion: Your life is in danger. Because you're a famous guy, anybody, even an uneducated gang member, can piece together the facts that you're a 12-year-old genius and your dad is an FBI official and head of the Joint Terrorism Task Force. You're going to have to take a leave of absence from Harvard and enter the FBI Witness Protection Program. Rick Bellamy has already made the arrangements. Obviously, you won't have any difficulty getting back into Harvard when this is all over. You'll move to a lovely house in Connecticut, a place we refer to as a 'safe-house.' Mom and I can visit you regularly, wearing disguises, of course. The FBI agents who will guard you are chosen for their friendly personalities as well as their ability to use a gun. And you can continue to work on your amazing projects."

"Oh, my God, Dad. When will all this happen?"

"Right now. Three agents from our local office are with me, and they'll help move your stuff into a van. I'll contact the administration at Harvard and let them know what's happening, without the details of course. Connecticut, here we come."

I wonder if Ellen Bellamy can come visit me, but I'm sure my dad would say no.

Chapter 13

ad was right. The house I'll be staying in is beautiful. It's in Darien, Connecticut, a pretty fancy town. The van pulled up to the gate and the driver typed in some numbers on his cell phone, causing the gate to open. Heck, I can design an optical recognition program to enable the guy to do that in the wink of an eye, but I'm getting ahead of myself. He then drove up a long driveway that continued around back. I noticed that a fence surrounded the plot in front of evergreen trees. Along the driveway were tall poles with objects on top, which I assumed were video and listening devices. I could see why they call this place a "safe house."

Mom was there to greet us. She wore a pistol on her waist, which always bothered me, but homicide detectives can't be too careful.

I noticed a bunch of people standing around in the huge den.

"Gladys Jackson, I believe you're the agent in charge of this house," my dad said. "Why don't you introduce us."

"As your dad just said, I'm agent Gladys Jackson, and this house is my responsibility. So, I'll be your *dorm mom,* if you will." We all laughed. Gladys, a tall, pretty, black lady, has a good sense of humor.

"This is agent Phil Burton and agent Nancy Carlin, my FBI

colleagues in charge of keeping you safe. And these two people are your fellow guests of the WPP, Mike and Alice Thompson, two NYPD officers who al-Qaeda would like to see dead, just as MS-13 would like to dispose of you, Leonardo."

My dad then introduced himself and my mom, who was busy yacking with her new NYPD friends. Cop or not, Mom's friendliness has a way of showing up.

"How's this for a coincidence?" Mom said. "The Thompsons and I know each other, having worked a few cases together. I've been wondering where you two went."

The house was huge, with three separate and completely private wings. That's good, I thought. I didn't like the idea of competing with other people to use the bathroom. Gladys showed me to my wing. Just the right size, with an extra bedroom off the living room, the place where I'd set up my computer. Mom and Dad can stay in the extra bedroom when they come to visit. And maybe Ellen Bellamy.

I felt kind of weird, no doubt about it. Just a few hours ago I sat in my dorm room at Harvard working on my novel-writing software and now I'm in the FBI Witness Protection Program. I made a mental note to plug some of these facts into the Austen database. I think she may come up with a good story.

Chapter 14

hepard Smith for *Fox News,* ladies and gentlemen. We've just received a disturbing report that a dormitory room at Harvard University was fire bombed with a highly flammable substance. The fire spread rapidly to the floor above and the entire dormitory has been evacuated. The FBI has requested that we not disclose the identity of the room's occupant. As of this time we don't know of any motive for the attack. In other news..."

Looks like Dad and the other FBI people made a good call about getting me into the Witness Protection Program. I couldn't believe that the day after I moved into the safe house, my dorm room at Harvard was firebombed. Thank God, nobody was killed. Obviously, MS-13 didn't get the memo that I had moved.

The FBI worked the heck out of my algorithm, and every day they would round up a few more gang members. My job wasn't done, because I needed to constantly tweak the program and add more facts and names that my research dug up. They continued to pay me my huge consulting fees, which I thought was cool. I invested most of it and I was getting to be kind of loaded with money with my stock trading talents. They still hadn't found the guy who torched my dorm room, but I was sure it's just a matter of time—I hoped.

I was still moving into my new home at the safe house, moving in mentally that is. The place kind of grew on me. I made it my own, hanging Ellen Bellamy pictures all over my walls. I set up two computers, a printer, and an extra monitor against one of the living room walls. I may be out of circulation, I thought, but no way would I let my projects get stale.

I made good friends with Mike and Alice Thompson, my fellow WPP "guests." They're a nice couple, about in their late 30s I figured. I got them hooked on *The Ellen Bellamy Show,* and we'd watch it together every day at 3 p.m. Because the Thompsons and I technically don't exist, we were free to talk about secret stuff. They loved it when I showed them how I came up with the MS-13 algorithm. The two of them had numerous encounters with the gang, and really freaked out when I showed them how a computer program can be used to fight crime. I also took a big liking to Gladys Jackson, our "dorm mom." She has a non-stop sense of humor and insists on calling me "Lombardo."

I was having a blast with Austen. I got special permission to connect with the Harvard mainframe remotely so I could tap into the huge Austen database. Harvard didn't know it was me, of course. They were told it was an FBI office renting the storage space. She (Austen) was still working on the book about the woman held hostage by a nut who thinks an alligator ate his car keys, and that's why they can't leave the God-forsaken house in the middle of nowhere. Here's the latest plot twist from Austen:

"Jerry," Dolores said to the nut, "do you still think an alligator ate your car keys."

"No," Jerry said. "I've been meaning to talk to you about that. It wasn't an alligator at all. It was a crocodile."

I had recently programmed Austen to come up with book titles.

She wanted to name the one she's working on, *See You Later Alligator.* Maybe not. This part of the program needs some work.

Chapter 15

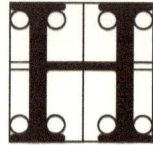ey, Lombardo, Secretary Bellamy is on the phone for you," Gladys said.

"Leonardo."

"Yeah, but Lombardo sounds more musical."

"Hi, Leonardo, Rick Bellamy here. We're on a secure line so feel free to talk. So, how are you finding life in the WPP?"

"The people here are great, and the house is beautiful, but I do feel like my life is on hold."

"Well, thank God we got you out of Harvard before your room was firebombed. I wanted to let you know that we found the guy—with no small help from your algorithm. He's an active member of the Boston branch of MS-13, or I should say he was an active member. Leonardo, not to exaggerate, but your computer work has revolutionized how we're dealing with the worst gang in history. We've been arresting hundreds of gang members a week. I can't believe they haven't figured out that we're on to them."

"Well, Mr. Secretary, I think people who torture and kill for fun aren't known for their brains."

"Hey, Leonardo, remember, the name's Rick."

"How's Mrs. Bellamy, I mean Ellen, Rick?" I *had* to ask.

"She's great. Ellen's looking forward to having you back on her show once you're out of the WPP. She's right here next to me. Say hello."

"Oh, hello Mrs. Mellany, I mean Mrs. Baloney, I mean Arlen, no—Ellen." Since when did I forget the English language? Ellen does things to my brain.

"Hi there, Leonardo. Great to hear your voice, my friend. I can't wait to have you back on my show."

I could swear I smelled her perfume through the phone.

"Me too," I managed to articulate.

"I'll let you and Rick catch up. So long, Leonardo. Hope to see you soon."

I kissed the phone. I cannot believe I kissed the friggin phone. I hoped they didn't hear it.

"I'll be signing off for now, Leonardo," Rick said. "Keep up the great work. Because of you, our country is a safer place."

It was nice of him to say that, but all I could think about was the sound of Ellen's voice—and the scent, imagined or not—of her perfume.

Chapter 16

had just woken up from a wonderful dream—about Ellen Bellamy of course. I woke up because I heard a loud sound that came from downstairs.

I opened the door of my suite to see if I could figure what was going on. Gladys ran, I mean sprinted, past my room with a pistol in her hand. Wow, for a tall lady she's fast as lightning. I don't think of myself as a hero, or in any way brave for that matter, but I think of Gladys as a good friend, and no way did I want anything bad to happen to her.

I had just stepped outside my room when agents Phil Burton and Nancy Carlin ran by, although not as fast as Gladys. Agent Burton carried an M16 rifle.

"Get back inside," Nancy Carlin said in a sort of shouted whisper.

Then came the sound of gunfire downstairs. Although I wasn't counting, my brain tallies up things whether I want it to or not. I heard a total of 20 gunshots. About a minute after the gunfire stopped, I heard Gladys yell, "Secure." Thank God she was okay. Five minutes later I heard a knock on my door.

"It's me, Lombardo, you can open the door," Gladys said. She didn't even sound out of breath. My dad always told me that FBI agents go through extremely rigorous physical training. I guess so.

Gladys hugged me. I think she sees me as her little brother. She smelled of gunpowder.

"Are you okay, honey?" she asked.

Am *I* okay? This lady just went through a gunfight and she wants to know if *I'm* okay. Next to Ellen Bellamy, I think Gladys is my favorite woman. I wonder if she'd like to date a little white kid.

"Come downstairs, Lombardo. We need to have a meeting."

"Leonardo," I said, hoping Gladys would find my remark funny. I was trying to cheer her up.

"Yeah, right," she said, as she put me in a friendly headlock.

"Don't look at that room," Agent Carlin said as I got to the bottom of the stairs. "It's gruesome. Five dead bodies."

I heard car doors slamming. A half dozen more FBI agents come running into the house. Gladys announced to everyone that we should gather in the large den, a good place for a meeting.

"Okay, everybody, listen up," Gladys said. "From the tattoos on those creeps, we know that they're from MS-13, which tells us they were no doubt after our friend Leonardo here."

"Don't you mean Lombardo?" I said.

"Shut up, Murphy," she said, laughing.

"Everybody can see why we call this place a safe house. I want to thank Agent Phil Burton, and Agent Nancy Carlin for their quick thinking and accurate shooting."

Gladys is way cool, no other way to put it. She led the charge into armed combat and there she was graciously thanking *other* people.

The night wore on as the agents kept asking us questions and jotting down notes. I guess this is what's called a crime scene.

I couldn't figure out what was going on with my emotions. For some reason I didn't feel fear. What I really felt was friendship for the people who saved me, especially my good friend Gladys. A few weeks ago, my dorm room at Harvard was firebombed and now five thugs show up, apparently wanting to kill me. Why do I feel calm? Maybe Mom and Dad, my brave parents, are rubbing off on me.

Chapter 17

he weeks went by and I began to notice something with my algorithm. The Internet "chatter" in the Caliche language had slowed to a trickle. Could they have figured out that the FBI is on to them? I doubt it. But then, nobody saw the attack on the safe house coming, not any of the FBI agents, not me, and not my algorithm. A computer program, no matter how well-designed, has its limitations.

I called my dad to compare notes. I told him that I saw fewer and fewer messages in Caliche, the code language of MS-13.

"Not only that, Leonardo, but crimes involving MS-13 are down to almost nothing. And Interpol has been making arrests in the hundreds as well overseas. Son, it seems to me that you personally destroyed the most violent gang in the world. I can't say often enough how proud I am of you. So is your mom. Hell, so is the entire law enforcement community."

"So, I guess I can concentrate on my novel-writing program."

"Well, maybe not. I was about to call you. Secretary Bellamy and I want to meet with you, as well as a guy from the CIA. We can be there in about an hour."

Wow. None other than my dad and Rick Bellamy are coming to

see me? And a guy from the CIA? I definitely think Austen should write a novel about my life in the past few weeks.

Chapter 18

saw a huge black SUV pull into the driveway. What is it about big black SUVs that government people seem to love? What's wrong with blue or maroon?

My dad, Rick Bellamy, and a tall Middle-Eastern looking guy walked through the back door. Gladys and I greeted them, and Dad introduced the other guy as Agent Gamal Akhbar, also known as Agent Charles Atkins, but everybody calls him Buster. We went up to the den in my suite for our meeting.

Gladys brought in a tray with coffee, sodas, and snacks. Although she holds an important executive position as the agent in charge of the safe house, Gladys is just plain friendly and likes to show hospitality. She also knows how to kill the enemy, as I saw recently.

"I know that your dad and you have discussed the shrinking of MS-13," Rick said. "I'm going to recommend that you don't return to Harvard this year, and your dad agrees with me. It only takes one person to attack you, and that's the last thing we want to happen. What occurred recently at this place convinced us, not to mention the firebombing of your room at Harvard. I'm going to let Buster take over the meeting, because he's what this get-together is all about."

"Leonardo, let me get right to the point," Buster said. "We need you. Your country needs you. What that amazing brain of yours did with the MS-13 problem has gotten the entire intelligence community paying attention. Are you familiar with the phrase, 'Terror Spectacular'?"

"Yes," I said, "as the words indicate it means a terrorist act of a large scale, such as 9/11, as opposed to small acts of murder or bombings."

"You hit it on the head, Leonardo, which is no surprise. So, here's the problem. I know that you've been deputized as an FBI agent and have top-secret clearance. What we'll discuss today is absolutely top secret. We've been getting indications for about six months from our various sources that something big may be in the planning stages. We're convinced that a large event is on the way. A terror spectacular doesn't need to be in one place. It could be a bunch of attacks in different locations that all add up to one huge act of terror. We've seen this happen in Europe and Japan. Like you, we rely heavily on computer algorithms to keep track of terror activities. But unlike you, we're not geniuses, smart maybe, but nothing like you. Secretary Rick and your dad have told us all about your program for tracking MS-13 conversations, using an odd Central American dialect called Caliche, I believe. I'm fluent in Arabic, and almost every terrorist we track speaks in an Arabic dialect or Farsi."

"Yes," I said. "My research convinced me that MS-13 used Caliche as a code language. So, I broke the code. Discovering and tracking terrorist plans in various Arabic dialects will be trickier. Trickier but doable."

"Leonardo, you just spoke the word I was looking for—'doable.' You have a rare gift for analyzing tons of complex data. And that's exactly what the CIA has, tons of complex data. Jack, Rick, I'm going to request that Leonardo come with me to Langley. I'll provide him with two bodyguards at all times. He can be housed right there at CIA headquarters, about as safe a safe house as you can find. Does that work for you, Leonardo?"

"If it's okay with my parents, it's okay with me. I don't want to see my country attacked."

"Jack, because this activity falls right in your lap as head of the Joint Terrorism Task Force, you may want to join us at Langley," Buster said.

"Are any other spies as young as me?"

"No, and none are as smart as you either."

Chapter 19

ur big black SUV dropped Secretary Rick at 26 Federal Plaza. Although his main office is in Washington, Rick prefers to work out of New York. I think he just wants to be near his beautiful wife, Ellen. Can you blame him?

Then our driver took us to Kennedy Airport.

"What time is our flight?" I asked.

"As soon as we get there," Buster said.

A CIA Gulfstream G650 awaited us at the airport. I guess that was what Buster meant when I asked what time our flight was. Wow. I read somewhere that the plane costs over $65 million. This was getting beyond cool.

During our flight, both my dad and Buster filled me in on just who Buster is.

"I may look like I ride a camel, Leonardo, but don't be fooled. I'm a jihadi's worst nightmare. I look like them and occasionally talk like them, but I'm not one of them. I get my looks from my Coptic Christian Egyptian parents. My job is to hunt down terrorists and kill them, I mean arrest them. Ignore what I just said about killing them. Remember, what I'm saying is top secret."

"CIA Director Bill Carlini, whom you'll meet, refers to Buster as a 'super spook,'" Dad said. "As you work with him, you'll see why."

After we touched down at the airport in Langley, a vehicle—a large black SUV, of course, picked us up for the short ride to CIA headquarters. As we walked through the beautiful entrance, I allowed myself to have yet another feeling of being hot stuff. Maybe the architect intended it that way, but the word I thought of when I saw the building was "imposing." It seemed that every doorway we entered let off beeping noises from the security system. It sounded like a video game arcade. Everybody seemed to know Buster and my dad. Even though they're both well-known, we were escorted by a security detail of guys who talked into their lapels.

It was 12:15, lunchtime, so we were led to the private dining room of Director William Carlini, which impressed the heck out of me. The view from Langley isn't exactly beautiful, but Carlini's dining room had a great view of a garden. Carlini was a nice guy, not what you'd expect from a top spy, not that I knew what to expect. He looked like a big-time business executive. I figured he was in his mid-50s, had sandy colored hair, and wore rimless glasses. I noticed a large button on his lapel, just like the security guys. I guess they like to communicate all the time. Maybe I can get one of those buttons. Cool.

"We've heard a lot about you, Leonardo, well actually everything about you," he said with a laugh. "You will find that we spies are always hungry for information. I'm not going to babble on about your excellent work on that MS-13 algorithm but let me just say that you pulled off one of the most important law enforcement successes our country has ever seen. You boxed in a crazed bunch of sadistic thugs and put them away with your facts. I know your dad here is used to beaming with pride about you, and he has every right to. You're a great American, Leonardo, somewhat young, but great nonetheless, and I'm delighted that you've agreed to join our team."

Wow, this guy knows how to make a kid feel important.

"Buster, why don't you give us a detailed rundown on what we've learned recently."

"When I met you in Connecticut, Leonardo," Buster said, "I gave you a brief survey of what we may be up against. Like you, we pay careful attention to algorithms because they can predict things that a human researcher might overlook. What we've been seeing in the past few weeks is Internet and email chatter—chatter like we've never seen before. We've learned over the years that an increase in chatter means that plans are underway. What those plans are, we don't know, because they don't speak or write anything specific, such as, 'Next Tuesday we're going to blow up the XYZ bridge.' They're not that clumsy."

"Buster, if I hear you correctly," I said, "it seems that they talk and write in code. If that's so, it's a matter of breaking the code, not that I'm saying it will be easy."

"Yes, Leonardo, they do speak in code. Over the years we've learned a lot about the code, but not nearly enough. Our analysts have identified 50 words that have specific alternate meanings. All the words are in Arabic. For example, we've discovered that the Arabic word 'cat' can also mean 'gun.'"

"I assume you've stored all of the phone conversations and texts and emails."

"Yes, and the phone conversations have been digitized in a text database which can be searched. But it's an enormous database."

"That's okay, Buster, I'm used to dealing with enormous amounts of data." I hoped he didn't think I was being a wise guy, but I felt I had to let him know my capabilities.

"There's another problem, Leonardo. You don't speak Arabic."

"As a matter of fact, I do, not as fluently as you, but I do have an elementary command of the language, especially vocabulary words."

"You never told me you speak Arabic, Leonardo," my dad said.

"I picked it up a few months ago. I didn't tell you because it never came up in conversation."

Buster and I then spent a couple of minutes chatting in Arabic.

"My God," Buster said. "you told us you have an elementary command of the language. I'd say you have an excellent command—you're basically fluent in Arabic."

"I'll continue to study the language. I've found that the way to break a code is to completely understand what goes into the code. We need to find a way to make sense of the chatter you referred to. If you'll pardon a dumb joke, we need to make the chatter matter."

"As I expected, Leonardo, you're way ahead of us already."

"So, I guess that for the near future this will be my new safe house."

"CIA Headquarters is a hell of a lot safer than a house in Connecticut."

Chapter 20

ood afternoon, ladies and gentlemen, and welcome to *The Ellen Bellamy Show*. My first guest today is Ronald Flemington, a former field operative with the Central Intelligence Agency. Mr. Flemington has worked in various CIA locations throughout the world, and recently retired after 25 years of service."

Oh my God, she looks gorgeous in that dress. I think the color is teal, which works perfectly with her sparkling blue eyes. I had just been shown to my room at the CIA and I was watching *The Ellen Bellamy Show* on my iPad. I decided to stream the show to my device so I wouldn't miss an episode.

"Mr. Flemington will be telling us about his new book, *Terrorism— The Main Event*."

Hey, this sounds interesting. Maybe I'll listen to the guy rather than just stare at Ellen. Well, I'll stare at her as well, but no harm in listening to a guest.

"What my book is about, Ellen, is the sad reality that we haven't seen anything yet from the organized groups of terrorism. The forces against us have never let down, but recently I see evidence that their operations are growing at an alarming rate. I predict in the book that in the very near future we will see a grouping of terror spectaculars that will make 9/11 look like a minor incident."

"How can you make that prediction, Mr. Flemington?" Ellen said. "I mean terrorists don't communicate their intentions before they pull off an event."

"It's a thing we call 'chatter,' Ellen. In other words, conversation and text traffic on the Internet and through emails. They don't announce what they intend to do, but the sheer volume of chatter tells us that something is in the works, and I suspect it will be a major event."

Hey, what's going on? This guy is talking about top secret stuff—on television, I thought. I picked up the phone.

"Buster, it's Leonardo. I need to show you something I think is urgent."

I put my iPad under my arm and ran as fast as I could to Buster's office. I have a DVR app so I record all of Ellen's shows, of course.

"Listen to what this guy is saying. I hit the restart key to play the show from the beginning. "He's talking about the stuff we discussed at lunch."

I played the segment for Buster. He slammed his hand on his desk and dialed his phone.

"Rick, it's Buster. That son of a bitch Flemington is on your wife's show talking about what we specifically forbade him from making public."

"I was just watching the show, Buster. I had the guy collared a couple of minutes ago. I always watch Ellen's show and I almost passed out when I saw that clown. I thought we had a court order against him."

"We *do* have a court order, but apparently Ellen's producers weren't aware of it."

"Ellen must be furious. Her producer no doubt stuck the guy in at the last minute as they often do, and Ellen probably knew nothing about him. It makes her look bad, even though it was her idiot producer who screwed up. At least we nailed the bastard before he got into too much detail. I intend to see Flemington behind bars. I mean holy shit, we grant the guy top secret clearance and then he spills the secrets to anybody with a television. I'll let you know what happens next. Thanks for the heads-up call."

"Don't thank me, thank Leonardo. He brought it to my attention."

"Of course," Rick said laughing. "Leonardo never misses an episode of *The Ellen Bellamy Show.*"

"Here's the spot where Secretary Bellamy had the guy stopped," I said to Buster.

We watched my rerun as Ellen grabbed her ear and announced a sudden station break, unlike her normal calm way of doing things. She looked upset, which got me upset.

"Thank you for joining us today, everybody. Ellen Bellamy signing off till tomorrow."

She took out her earpiece and speed dialed a number on her phone.

"Rick, what was that all about?"

"Your guest was spreading top secret information, in direct violation of a court order the CIA got against him. I recommend, hon, that you don't let your producers slip a fast one by you. It' standard practice at all networks, including yours, to vet anybody who will be talking about a matter involving national security."

"I'm sorry, honey."

"Don't be ridiculous, it's not your fault. Maybe CBS should hire Leonardo Murphy to design a system to vet guests."

"Not a bad idea."

Chapter 21

miss my FBI friend Gladys from Connecticut and I think she misses me too. When people go through a major trauma like we did at the safe house, friendships tend to grow and last. At least that's what my parents told me. Gladys and I communicate regularly by email—secure email, of course. My new code name, which I find ridiculous, is Xray Zulu. Gladys, with her great sense of humor, always begins a message to me with, "Dear Xray." She always ends a message by saying, "Looking right through you."

I enjoy working with the IT guys at the CIA. They're really smart and pleasant to work with. Well, somewhat smart. They do understand the importance of algorithms, and why they're necessary to spot trends in huge amounts of data. They understand that with the gigantic world of terror we need to track information. What they don't get is the significance of what they're looking at.

"Hey, Leonardo," said Jim Locklear, the head of the IT unit. "You've been working with us for four days. Come up with anything new yet?"

"As a matter of fact, I have, Jim. I've come up with a new algorithm, but I wanted to test it a bit before I showed it to you. I don't know if it's any better than the one you're using, but it's worth a look. I was being overly polite (and struggling valiantly not to be an asshole). Their algorithm was terrible, a sophomoric program that was obviously slapped together by a committee. Jim was being friendly with me and I wanted to keep it that way. As Grandpa Ezekiel always told me, if you make a person feel stupid, he will become your enemy.

"Well, give me an overview of your new design," Jim said.

"First, I took all of the words that we see coming up in the 'chatter.' I then assigned a value to those words based on how many times they're used, and also to the meaning of the words as they're used in conjunction with other words. I've also isolated words in classic Arabic from those in rural dialects. After studying the language for a couple of months, I'm starting to get the hang of it."

"Buster tells me you already have an excellent command of the language, Leonardo. Now remember our first meeting a few days ago. I told you that we try to come up with constant hypotheses to see where the data is taking us. So, any predictions to share with me?"

"Yes, Jim, and it's pretty upsetting. First let's talk about timing. This is the month of April. Seven months from now we can expect some pretty spectacular stuff—in early November. I think we'll be looking at a total of 30 different events across the country. All the attacks will involve pentaerythritol tetranitrate, or PETN, which, as you know, is one of the most powerful non-nuclear explosives. It's a key ingredient in Semtex, the plastic explosive and the one I believe will be used. You may remember that a Semtex weapon, weighing about 12 ounces, brought down that Boeing 747 over Lockerbie, Scotland a few years ago. As far as targets, I'm still working on that issue, but I can make an educated prediction that the targets will be commuter trains, airplanes, buildings, and possibly cruise ships."

"Buster, it's Jim Locklear. I think you should come down to my office. I'm with Leonardo, and he has me shitting a brick."

Buster showed up in Jim's office in less than two minutes. Wow. I heard that Buster moves fast, and I just saw proof of it.

"Leonardo, tell Buster what you just told me."

I did. Buster may not be a computer geek, but he catches on fast with technical stuff. He and Jim may not understand computer science like I do, but they both knew that answers were lurking in the data. I explained how I came up with the algorithm, going into more detail than I did with Jim.

"And you did this in four days?" Buster said.

"Well, I had a great head start with the work that Jim and his people did before I got here," I politely lied.

"Leonardo, if you have an answer to my next question I shall personally nominate you for sainthood. Here's the question. How can we detect Semtex before it explodes?"

"Well, this saint won't be marching in, Buster." I thought my comment was quite witty.

They didn't.

I figured I'd better get to the point without being a wiseass.

"Yes, Semtex can be detected before detonation. After the Lockerbie bombing the International Civil Aviation Organization drummed up support to require that Semtex and other plastic explosives be treated with a detection substance, known as a taggant, which sets off vapors that a dog or a special device can sense. But the big problem is that it can't be detected from very far. If you don't suspect the presence of the explosive, you probably won't find it before it detonates. So, let's look at some numbers, which are pretty scary. As I said before, the plastic explosive device that caused the Lockerbie disaster was only 12 ounces. If my algorithm numbers are close to correct, there will be 30 explosion sites. That's only 360 ounces, or 22.5 pounds, about the size of a bag of kitty litter—spread over 30 locations across the country—and we don't know where those sites are. So, as a practical matter, detection is impossible. Our only hope is, as I tweak my algorithm and add more data, that you and the other agents can come up with some leads."

"Hey, Buster," Jim said, "I don't know about you but I'm feeling confident. Leonardo came up with his amazing predictions in four days. If he's right, we have seven months to track down the bombers."

"Leonardo, I'm keeping your sainthood application handy," Buster said.

Chapter 22

Mom and Dad visit me at least once a month at my new home in Langley, Virginia. My apartment was spacious and comfortable, although not as nice as the place in Connecticut. This afternoon they'll be here to celebrate my 13th birthday. Today I'm officially a teenager, armed with the power to turn into an asshole on a moment's notice. I keep a picture of Grandpa Ezekiel in my wallet and look at it regularly.

My folks arrived at 2:45, just in time to join me in watching *The Ellen Bellamy Show*. Ellen, who looked glowing in a soft yellow dress, began with a light segment about a guy who came up with a revolutionary way to double a tomato plant's yield without adding chemicals. Revolutionary? I came up with that idea three years ago, but I didn't publicize it. Ellen's producers should bounce ideas off me. Better yet, I could meet privately with Ellen. But there I was at Langley, the country's youngest spy, without the ability to venture forth on my own because I was still in the Witness Protection Program. This was becoming less cool every day.

At 4:30 we went to Director Carlini's office for my birthday party. Buster was there, along with Jim Locklear and a few others from the IT department. Mom and Dad were there too. Dad knows almost everybody at CIA headquarters because of his position as head of the Joint Terrorism Task Force. We're on the secure line at least once a day. Dad really digs my algorithms.

As everybody sang happy birthday, an aide walked in with my birthday cake. It had gray lumpy icing, which looked unappetizing. "Why gray?" I asked. Buster laughed and said it was meant to represent the "gray matter" in my brain.

CIA humor can be kind of lame.

Everybody took turns giving a little speech in my honor. If I heard the words "bright young man" one more time I thought I'd barf. But they're all nice people even though they embarrass me with their constant flattery.

After the party, Director Carlini announced that there would be a brief meeting so I could update everybody on my algorithm. Mom didn't need to be asked to leave the room. She just announced that she was going to the third floor to visit an old friend. Even though mom's a big-shot chief homicide detective, she didn't have the necessary "need to know" about the subject of our meeting. Mom is way cool without even trying.

"Leonardo," Director Carlini said, "please bring us up to date on the status of your algorithm. Has anything major changed since we met last week?"

"It's been three weeks since I've been working on the program, sir. I predict that by this coming Friday I'll have some exciting news, really exciting, and also kind of scary. For now, I can say that I'm convinced that my predictions of timing and number of bombings are accurate within a small percentage of possible error, but I warn you that the timing is crucial. If my timing prediction is off by even a small degree, it could mean disaster."

I hoped they listened to my warning about the timing of the

events. Sometimes I get the feeling that they think my algorithms are infallible. They're not.

Chapter 23

Director Carlini called another meeting to check on my algorithm's progress. He introduced me to a new guy I hadn't met before, CIA Agent Mark Donovan. Director Carlini said that Donovan was a new "station chief," meaning that he's the guy in charge of the CIA station at headquarters, although Carlini has overall supervision of the agency. Carlini assigned the terror-spectacular matter I was working on to Donovan. I don't like to jump to conclusions about people, but this Donovan guy struck me as being pompous and thick headed, somebody who doesn't care for the opinions of others. He wears a smirk on his face as if it was a scar. Maybe I'm wrong. I hope I am.

"So, tell us, Leonardo, anything new with our friendly algorithm?"

"Yes, sir, Director Carlini. I've been waiting for this meeting to make my announcement. I've discovered the names of five key people involved in planning the November bombings. Of course, I won't announce the names here, according to protocol, but I will hand them to Buster."

Everybody just stared at me open mouthed.

Then Buster reached into his pocket and withdrew a piece of paper, which he unfolded and pointed to.

"What's that, Buster?" Carlini asked.

"It's Leonardo's application for sainthood, which I'm filling out for him."

Everybody cracked up. I'm really getting to like Buster. I think we're becoming good friends. Because of that new station chief, Donovan, I need all the friends I can get.

"Buster, without announcing the names," the director said, "why don't you plug them into that computer against the wall and let us know if our database recognizes any of them."

Buster entered the names. Wow, he types almost as fast as me.

Buster turned and looked at us.

"Every name on Leonardo's list is on our watchlist. Leonardo, you're amazing."

"I've added a few lines of code to my algorithm to constantly track those names and see if any new names show up," I said. "I hate to sound overly optimistic, but I think we have this problem under control. I hope I'm not overstepping my bounds by asking this question, but isn't it just a matter of tracking these people down and arresting them?"

"Young man," Mark Donovan said, (I hate it when people call me *young man*, especially when they do it with a snide grin and a smirk.) "The one thing you need to learn about the intelligence business is patience. I want you to keep tweaking your program and try to see if you come up with additional names. According to your prediction, we have a few months before the attacks. Let's use those months productively. As we expected, you've gotten us a lot further down the road than we had ever hoped. Take us further, young man."

Chapter 24

The months went by. I guess I shouldn't feel nervous, but I do. That guy Donovan insists that spooks need to be patient and let the evidence take them where it needs to. My job is to work the computer and continuously tweak the data. The guys in the field, like Buster, are the ones who will make things happen, or stop them from happening. Heck, I don't even know how to shoot a gun. But it's the first week in October, and my prediction is that the Semtex attacks will happen in November. What if my predictions are off a bit? Is thirteen years old too young to develop an ulcer? I needed to calm myself down. I decided to call Buster, and I didn't care what the new "station chief" thinks.

"Buster, I'm probably being out of line, but this patience business has me worried. I think I saw that on your face too. A computer algorithm is nothing more than a digital method of analyzing data—it's not sacred scripture. What if the terror planners *purposely* leaked the timing knowing that it was wrong? My algorithm can't tell the difference between information and *disinformation*. Besides that, what if they simply decide to move the date of the planned attacks up? It isn't my responsibility to say this, Buster, but I think it's time to act."

"Leonardo, I share your concerns, big time. That station chief Donovan is technically my boss, but I get the impression that he sometimes thinks with his biceps. You're absolutely right. What if the enemy is leaking us the wrong timing information? If it was my call, I'd bust the sons of bitches right now. I'm going to ask to meet with Director Carlini and get this concern out in the open. I'm going to talk to your dad too. He also seemed skeptical about Donovan's lecture on patience. It may get me fired, but this is too important. As you put it so well, if your timing prediction is off by even a little bit it could mean disaster. Thanks for the heads up, my friend."

Chapter 25

Oh, great, it's 2:45, just 15 minutes to *The Ellen Bellamy Show*. Watching Ellen always calms me down. Well, sort of. I felt better after my phone call with Buster yesterday. Now I know he shares my concern about us exercising too much patience. I gave them the names, and I even found the addresses. Why the heck don't they just get arrest warrants and be done with it?

"Good afternoon ladies and gentlemen, and welcome to *The Ellen Bellamy Show*. My guest today is Dr. Alvin Brady, a professor of computer science at Harvard."

Cool. I took one of Professor Brady's courses in my first semester. I got a lot of my Jane Austen program ideas from him.

"Professor, please tell us about the latest inroads in the fascinating science of artificial intelligence. A few months back I interviewed a young man named Leonardo Murphy, who I understand was a student of yours at Harvard. He discussed a program that he called Jane Austen, software that tells a computer how to write a novel."

Wow, this is beyond cool. If it weren't against CIA rules I'd do a call-in.

"Yes, Ellen, Leonardo was one of the best students I ever taught.

Sometimes I thought he was teaching *me*. He's on a leave of absence from Harvard, and he seems to have gone into seclusion for some reason. He's probably reworking Einstein's general theory of relativity."

Oh, my goodness. When people like him say such nice things about me, it takes a lot of effort not to be an asshole.

"Yes, Leonardo is one brilliant kid, professor."

The show was almost over. Time flies when you're being flattered.

Ellen grabbed her ear, a serious look suddenly coming over her face. She looked frightened.

"Pardon me professor, but we have major breaking news to report. We go now to Bill Tomkins to fill us in on a story that's happening right now."

"Thanks, Ellen. We've just received a horrifying report of a major train derailment just outside of downtown Chicago on the city's north side. According to eyewitness reports there was a huge explosion before the train flew off the tracks. Jack Monroe from our affiliate station in Chicago is on the scene."

Oh, my God, I thought. I can't believe what I'm seeing. Could I be watching the start of my predicted bomb attacks? I think that Donovan jerk was being way too patient. I hope he's watching TV.

"Jack Monroe reporting for *CBS* in Chicago, folks. If you look behind me you can get some idea of the devastation that just occurred, a scene of horror that is still unfolding. The commuter train was traveling on an overhead trestle when the explosion occurred. If you look at that tall building next to the track you can see that almost every window has been blown out. A police detective I just spoke to says that he thinks it was a plastic explosive, most likely Semtex, because of the power of the blast. You may recall that a small amount of Semtex brought down a 747 over Lockerbie, Scotland a few years ago. As you can see, the entire train of 10 cars has been derailed. I'm afraid that there will be an enormous loss of life, not only on the train, but also on the ground below the trestle."

"Jack, sorry to interrupt. This is Bill Tomkins in New York. I've just received word that a 747 coming in for a landing at Kennedy International Airport has fallen out of the sky. Witnesses say that they saw a huge explosion as the plane was on its final approach. The aircraft then crashed into Jamaica Bay."

Tomkins grabbed his earpiece, a look of fright on the guy's face. Obviously, somebody was yelling stuff into his ear. I felt like throwing up, but I held it in.

"Ladies and gentlemen, I'm getting a report of another train derailment, this one in Minneapolis. Wait, there's more. I'm told that another plane, a Boeing 737, has crashed outside of Orlando, Florida.

"I also just received a report that the Norwegian Line cruise ship Sea Melody was approaching a pier in Bermuda when a huge explosion destroyed her navigation bridge. I've also been told that the engine room was bombed. The ship then collided with the pier where hundreds of people awaited her. Two more explosions were heard.

"Now I'm getting a report of a gigantic blast in the Willis Tower, formerly known as the Sears Tower, on the edge of Chicago's loop. It's the second tallest building in the United States. Folks, please bear with me. My producers, the people shouting in my earpiece, are barely able to keep up with what's happening. I'm going to take a deep breath and give you the information as I get it.

"I now hear of another explosion and train derailment in Philadelphia, and yet another on the Metrolink in Los Angeles. I'm now being told of another cruise ship that has exploded next to her pier in Miami. My friends, today's events are starting to make 9/11 look like a fender bender. Ladies and gentlemen, our nation is under attack."

Jim Locklear, head of the IT Department, walked into the office.

"I hope you're not going to lecture me about being patient, Jim," I said. I was being a bit of a snot, but I didn't care. My country was coming apart at the seams, and my algorithm missed it by almost a month—and I warned everybody about that very possibility.

"Leonardo, I don't think of you as a kid, I think of you as a colleague. You and I and the others in my department are the computer geeks at the CIA. We don't get to call the shots. The folks upstairs do. For the past few months I heard you complaining that we were being *too* patient. I heard our new boss, Donovan, lecture you that we all need to be *more* patient. Well, the enemy was a few steps ahead of us, as we're just finding out. I think they *fed* us wrong information, disinformation, to put us where we are today, just like you cautioned us. I heard you warn anybody who would listen that we were basing our plans on the assumption that the attacks would happen a month from now. You even sounded the alarm that we may have been fed the wrong timing information. So, you spoke, but not enough people listened. We assumed the enemy was stupid. They're not. Totally evil, but not stupid. What are your thoughts, my friend?"

"One of the many great pieces of advice my grandad Ezekiel gave me was to never say 'I told you so.' I won't say that to Director Carlini. I definitely won't say it to you, Jim, because you agreed with my concerns. And I won't say it to Buster either, because he understood what I was talking about, and so did my father. The White House handed down a directive that this would be a CIA operation, not FBI. So, I guess we learned a big lesson today. Computer algorithms can give you guidance, but they can't totally predict reality. Grandpa Ezekiel lectured me that I should never be an asshole. I wish that Grandpa Ezekiel had a chance to meet that guy Donovan, the biggest asshole I've ever met."

"Leonardo, you're only thirteen years old, but I think you're the most mature person I've encountered, not just smart, mature. I just want you to know that it's an honor to work with you. Hey, let's go into the lounge and watch the news reports on TV. We don't have anything else to do."

Jim Locklear and I parked ourselves in front to the TV. After 10 minutes, I wasn't sure it was a good idea. We both agreed that what we were watching was sickening. The news networks could barely keep up with the unfolding catastrophe. Jim was clicking from station to station. We watched burning airplanes, derailed trains, exploding cruise ships, and bombed out buildings. Any one of the events would be an all-consuming news report. Put them all together and it was like watching a horror movie.

"Oh, dear God," Jim said. "please tell me I'm not seeing that."

We watched as the gigantic Willis Tower collapsed to the ground, taking two nearby buildings with it.

My algorithm seems to have gotten one thing right—the number of attacks. All told, 29 bombs detonated, close to my estimate of 30. Thirteen planes crashed, seven trains, six buildings destroyed, and three cruise ships bombed. I was more furious than I'd ever been in my life. I mean who did that clown Donovan think he was dealing with, a cute little genius? If he thought I was such a friggin genius, why didn't he listen to me? The reports are still coming in, but over 59,000 people died. My God, that's more Americans than died in the Vietnam War—all because spooks are supposed to be patient? My patience has hit its limit. If they want me to work here anymore, and I'm not sure *I* do, they better start listening to my answer when they ask a question. I've had it with this bullshit. Oh, great. Now I'm even using cusswords, which I never do.

Chapter 26

"Jack, I'm worried about Leonardo," Rebecca Murphy said. "He's only 13 and he's under more pressure than the next 100 adults in line. As brilliant as he is, I think this CIA crap is too much for him. And that new station chief idiot didn't even listen to him when he sounded the alarm about the timing of the attacks. I know this because Leonardo told me. I don't think his top-secret oath would let him keep it from his mother. And I know he warned you too."

"Yes, he did. If the White House didn't insist that the operation be strictly for the CIA I would have sounded the alarm. Hell, my conscience won't let me alone. I should have gone right to the White House and raised hell. But I didn't, and we got hit by an unimaginable terror attack. Dear God, 59,000 people dead. My title is Director of the Joint Terrorism Task Force. But I sure as hell didn't do much directing, did I?"

"Don't dare blame yourself, honey. That was the president's call and he made it. Remember what he told you? 'This is a job for the CIA.' Yeah, right. If *you* were running the show this shit never would have happened. Let's get Leonardo the hell out of there, Jack. He's only 13 and he should go back to Harvard—where he belongs, not in a spy agency run by assholes."

"I think Bill Carlini wants Leonardo there."

"Well fuck Bill Carlini. If he wants him there, why the hell didn't he listen to him instead of that Donovan shithead?"

Chapter 27

just turned 20 and I'm about to get a PhD in physics from Harvard University. I graduated with my BS two years ago at age 18 after a two-year leave of absence so I could pursue a brief career as a CIA spy. Although it's been seven years, I still can't forget the horrors of October 7, better known as 10/7. I wish I could get those images from the TV out of my mind. I'm blessed with a photographic memory, but I just wish the photos would go away.

One of the many things Grandpa Ezekiel taught me was never to *overlearn* a lesson from something. In other words, don't make a firm rule for yourself based on one event. But having said that, I will never allow myself to become involved in a bureaucracy again. I kept warning the "powers that be" about something that should have been obvious. I tried to get it through their thick friggin skulls that if my timing prediction was off, the result would be cataclysmic. But no, spies must show patience. Right. Explain that to the families of the 59,000 people killed on 10/7. After the attacks, the CIA did manage to find the bombers. Why not? I gave them the names that my algorithm disclosed. Although the government never admitted it, I've heard that the CIA agents simply killed the perpetrators instead of arresting them. When people are angry, and there were a lot of angry spooks after 10/7, they often ignore the rules, such as the United States Constitution. Assholes.

The only good thing about all this is that my dad, as head of the

Joint Terrorism Task Force, personally convinced Director Carlini to fire that bozo Donovan. I'm glad Dad ran out of patience.

I was having lunch with my parents near police headquarters at One Police Plaza, aka 1PP, after I returned from Harvard. We had always stayed in touch over the years, but it was great to see them in person.

"So, Leonardo, or should I say *Doctor* Leonardo, what do you plan to do next now that you have your PhD?" Mom asked.

"I think I'll join the Navy."

"Don't be a wise guy."

"No, I'm serious. The Navy has always fascinated me, especially when I listen to the stories that you and Dad tell about your experiences as naval officers. I love that story about how you two met on a ship during a general quarters drill. You both had the same battle station. That is so cool I think I'll have Austen write a novel about it. I'm not thinking about making the Navy a career, but I think a few years at sea would be exciting. I'm sure I'll come up with some new project ideas."

An uncomfortable silence followed my words. Mom kept stirring her coffee, and dad sat there saying nothing. Finally, he broke the silence.

"I love your idea, Leonardo," Dad said. "As if your mom and I aren't proud of you already, I think the idea of our son following our footsteps is wonderful. God knows, the Navy can use a brain like yours."

"Dad's right, Leonardo. With a PhD in physics from Harvard you have your pick of what you want to do. I think a few years in the Navy will do you wonders. It will make us even prouder than we are now. When are you going to make this happen?"

"After we finish lunch, I'm going to the Navy Recruiting Station on Chambers Street. I just wanted to bounce the idea off you two first."

"Anchors aweigh, honey," Mom said.

Chapter 28

I just finished my 12 weeks at Officer Candidate School (OCS) in Newport, Rhode Island, and received my bars as an ensign in the United States Navy. I found the course work to be a snap, and I finished first in my class. I'm not used to being structured, but I found out that there was something rewarding about following somebody else's ideas for a change. I got my orders this morning, and I'll report to the *USS Gerald R. Ford* at Naval Station Norfolk in Virginia tomorrow.

I checked in with the ship's personnel officer this morning and was assigned a stateroom that I'll share with another ensign. I was having lunch by myself in the Officer's Club when a beautiful woman wearing the bars of a lieutenant walked up to my table.

"You're Leonardo Murphy, aren't you?"

I had hoped for some anonymity, but my face has a way of showing up in newspapers.

"Yes, ma'am," I said. "I was hoping nobody would recognize me."

"I'm Lieutenant Meg Fenton. Please have lunch with my husband

and me. Our table is in the corner. My husband is Admiral Harry Fenton. He's the Commanding Officer of Carrier Strike Group 14. The *USS Gerald R. Ford* is his flagship. I heard that you are assigned to the *Ford*."

"You know that already?"

"I'm Admiral Harry's chief of staff. Very little happens around here without me knowing about it."

"My God, I just realized who you are, America's favorite couple— America's Twofer as the president has called you. Wow. Admiral and Lieutenant Fenton. It's an honor to meet you ma'am."

"Please call me Meg. May I call you Leo?"

"Leonardo, ma'am, I mean Meg."

"Come on, Leonardo, I want you to meet Harry."

I remembered reading about Admiral Fenton and his lovely wife. A lot of pundits say that Harry Fenton is the greatest fighting admiral since Nimitz. Meg was a former big-time securities executive I recalled, but she loves the Navy more than making money. She's also an ace fighter pilot, I've read. I also read that despite the Navy's reluctance to have a husband and wife serve on the same ship, the Bureau of Naval Personnel regularly made an exception for the Fentons. Assigning officers is always done with "the good of the service" as the top priority, and that goal was amply met with the Fentons. And I was about to have lunch with them. Cool.

"Honey, I mean Harry, I mean Admiral, Ensign Murphy here is

the guy I thought he was, Leonardo Murphy. From everything I've read about him, he's got more brainpower than the combined crew of the *Ford*, and he's stationed on the ship."

I couldn't believe he stood up to shake my hand. An admiral standing to shake the hand of a lowly ensign? From what I've read about him he's a real gentleman. Admiral Harry is my height, 6'2" but he seemed taller. I read that he's about 42 years old, but he looks much younger.

"Pleasure to meet you, Ensign. Mind if I call you Leonardo? I read somewhere that you don't like to be called Leo."

"Of course, sir, it's a pleasure to meet you too. I've read a lot about you and Lieutenant Meg."

"If what I've read about you is true, you probably remember everything you've read about us. I guess you're familiar with *The Maltese Incident*, the little time travel journey where I met my lovely wife here."

"Yes, sir, the most amazing story I ever heard. I read your book about the experience, *The Maltese Incident*. You traveled back to the time of the dinosaurs, and you proved that time travel is no longer just a matter of science fiction, but a real technical phenomenon."

"Coming from a Harvard physicist, Leonardo, I'll take that as a vote of confidence. Have you ever studied time travel?"

"Yes, sir. I wrote a book about the Einstein-Rosen Bridge, commonly known as a wormhole. I'm fascinated by the subject."

"That doesn't surprise me. From what I've heard about you there's very little you haven't written about. So, what brings you to the Navy, Leonardo? From what I've read about you, you're the smartest person in the world. Do you think you'll find enough to challenge your brain on a warship?"

"Both my parents were naval officers, sir. They actually met on a ship during a general quarters drill where they both had the same battle station. We're a very close family, so it seemed natural for me to follow in their footsteps. Also, I think of myself as a patriot."

"What department are you assigned to, Leonardo?" Meg asked.

"Communications. The detailer who gave me my orders felt it would be a good assignment for me."

"Harry?" Meg said. That's all she said as she stared at him. I had read this about these two. They're so close they can communicate with just a word and a glance.

"You're right as usual, hon." Admiral Harry said. My God, she hadn't said anything. She just looked at him and said his name, but there he was, answering a question she didn't ask.

"Leonardo, I'm reassigning you to my staff as an admiral's aide. You'll work closely with Meg, my chief of staff and right hand. I need a brain like yours on my staff. And you'll get to wear a fancy epaulette on your shoulder like Meg. Do you know anything about the *Ford*? I realize that you were assigned just yesterday, but I was just wondering where you are in your knowledge about our ship."

"Yes, Admiral, I did some reading on my way here, not just the Ford, but the other ships in CSG-14."

I then spent the next five minutes telling them everything I knew about the *Ford*, including her firepower, speed, electronics, aircraft, defenses, nuclear power plant, and navigation. I also discussed the other four ships in the group in detail. They just stared at me.

"Welcome aboard, pal," Admiral Harry said.

Chapter 29

he *USS Gerald R. Ford* is an amazing ship. The *Ford* launched in 2013 and was formally commissioned on July 22, 2017. The ship is the first of the *Ford* Class aircraft carriers, which will eventually replace the *Nimitz* Class carriers. Her total cost, including research and development, was about 18 billion dollars. The *Ford* is the largest ship ever launched, with a length of 1,106 feet and a beam of 134 feet at the waterline and 256 feet on the flight deck. She displaces over 100,000 tons. The ship is powered by two nuclear reactors, and her cruising range is virtually unlimited.

After two weeks at sea, I was happy that I decided to join the Navy. My job is a big one, aide to Admiral Fenton, or Admiral Harry as I usually call him. He and Meg are the closest couple I've ever encountered, and I include my parents. Just as the first time I met them, I would often see them having "conversations" without speaking a word. Meg is one of the smartest people I've ever met, and I've met quite a few. She's also beautiful. If she wasn't Admiral Harry's wife I knew where my efforts would focus, even though she's almost 15 years older than me. Don't be an asshole I reminded myself often.

My job on the ship, as well as Meg's, is to assist Admiral Harry to command Carrier Strike Group 14, not just the *Ford*. Besides the *Ford*, the group consists of the guided missile cruiser *USS Vicksburg* (CG-69), two Arleigh Burke class destroyers, the *USS Oscar Austin* (DDG 79), and the *USS Arleigh Burke* (DDG-51).

As I usually do when I take on a project, I memorized everything about every ship in the group. The admiral knows that if he has a question, I have the answer. On Meg's recommendation, I also addressed myself to the onboard computer database, which was a surprising mess, or at least it seemed so to me. The database includes information on every crewmember of every ship in the group, as well as detailed information on every weapon and aircraft, but a lot of it was incomplete and sketchy.

One day, Admiral Harry asked me if I'd like to accompany Meg on one of her training flights. Like all pilots, Meg is required to fly regularly to maintain her proficiency. I've learned, in a short time, that when Admiral Harry makes a suggestion, it's an order. So, I suited up in flight gear, and climbed aboard an F/A 18 Super Hornet, Meg's favorite plane. When I was a kid, I loved to go to amusement parks and hop on the wildest rides available. No roller coaster can compare to the excitement of launching off a flight deck in a Super Hornet, a monster of an airplane. It has an internal 20 mm rotary cannon and can carry air-to-air missiles and air-to-surface weapons. It can carry additional fuel in up to five external fuel tanks. The plane can be configured as an airborne tanker by adding an external air refueling system. It can fly at Mach 1.8, about 1,190 MPH. Think of a rocket with wings.

"What do you think, Leonardo, would you like to learn to fly one of these?" Meg said as we leveled off after climbing to 1,000 feet.

"How long does flight school take?" I asked.

"Six weeks. We'll be in port for two months installing a new weapons system starting next month. I'm sure Admiral Harry will recommend you."

"I want to see how you maneuver this thing first, and then we can talk further after we land."

Our plane, along with two other Hornets, would now go through some drills.

"Hang on, Leonardo. If you can stomach our next few maneuvers, you'll know if you want to be a pilot or not."

Meg had command of this flight, and she began to give orders to the other two Hornets. We went into a straight climb to 15,000 feet. We then turned and dove straight down, leveling off at 5,000 feet. I was enjoying myself. Actually, I loved it. Me, a jet pilot? We'll see.

"We're about to begin our approach for a landing, Leonardo. Hold on to your helmet."

"Is it as much fun as taking off?"

"Actually, it sucks, but it's something I have to do."

One of a pilot's most critical jobs when coming in for a carrier landing is to "call the ball," indicating to the landing crew on the flight deck that he, or in this case, she, has a visually accurate view of the "meatball." The ball, or meatball, is an orange orb of light emitted from the optical landing system on the carrier's flight deck. A green horizontal row of lights (known as the datum) indicates proper glide slope. If the ball is below the datum, the aircraft is low, and if it's above the datum, the plane is high. When the meatball is in proper view, the pilot repeatedly says, "Roger Ball."

I listened as Meg repeated "Roger Ball." Our tailhook caught the arresting wire and we went from 150 miles an hour to zero in a couple of seconds. I can see why Meg says that landing on a carrier deck sucks. It's scary. If the pilot loses sight of the ball, it can mean disaster. But it was kind of fun—as long as somebody else was at the controls.

Chapter 30

Admiral Harry and Meg convinced me that I should get my wings. When I was in OCS they held a special meeting to recruit pilots. I remember the officer in charge of the presentation saying, "If you're thinking of becoming a pilot, the first requirement is that you want it badly." That got me thinking about it. My flight with Meg convinced me.

I told Admiral Harry that I would like to continue as his aide after flight school. He made it clear to me that he also wanted me to stay on and told me that getting my wings would make me a more valuable aide. The thought occurred to me that I may be reassigned when I got my wings. Meg told me not to worry. The Bureau of Naval Personnel, not to mention the White House, listens to Admiral Harry so I shouldn't be concerned.

So, I reported to flight school at Naval Air Station, Pensacola, Florida. The six weeks went by fast, especially the academic part which I breezed through. The school ended with my first solo flight and landing on an aircraft carrier. The plane I trained on was a T-45 Goshawk, a twin seat jet. Bringing it in for a landing on the *USS Nimitz* was an experience I'll never forget. The first thing I did after I landed was call my parents. Mom, being Mom, was scared as hell that I'd be flying jets. But she also loved the idea. Go figure.

I requested and was accepted into the training program for the F/A-18 Super Hornet, adding additional time to my flight training before I reported back aboard the *Ford*.

The *Ford* was still tied up at Norfolk, so I didn't have the thrill of landing on her deck to show off my new wings.

When I reported back aboard, the OOD told me that I was expected at the Officer's Club. Typical of the Fentons, Admiral Harry and Meg threw a party for me to celebrate my earning my wings as a Navy pilot. I realized that I had discovered two friends for life.

Chapter 31

Two years later.

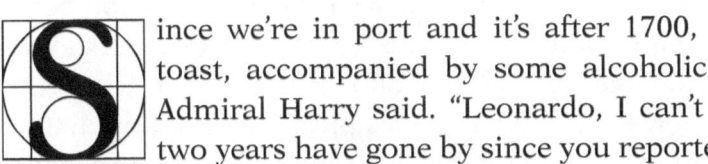ince we're in port and it's after 1700, I propose a toast, accompanied by some alcoholic beverages," Admiral Harry said. "Leonardo, I can't believe that two years have gone by since you reported aboard. It seems like just yesterday when Meg introduced us at the O Club. So, by the power vested in me by the United States Navy Bureau of Naval Personnel, and because you have the required time in grade, I hereby promote you to lieutenant junior grade. Ladies and gentlemen, let's raise our glasses to a fine young officer, Lieutenant JG Leonardo Murphy, the man who turned our IT department upside down and made it the best in the Navy. And he even got his wings."

We were having a full staff meeting of a dozen people.

"Okay folks, Leonardo, Meg, and I are about to go into executive committee. That is all. Carry on."

I thought it was totally cool how Admiral Harry considers Meg and me as his executive committee.

"Even though we have a nuclear power plant," Meg said, "I've figured out a way we can cut down on electricity usage."

"How's that?" Admiral Harry asked.

"We can turn off our computers. With Leonardo here, we don't need computers."

We laughed. Meg knows how to use her sense of humor to throw a compliment.

"Keep the jokes coming, Meg. After what I have to tell you both, we're going to need some laughs. I just received a communication from Naval Intelligence that our onboard terrorism problems have not gone away. It seems they've picked up a lot of chatter recently about a planned incident right here on the *Ford*. Leonardo, God knows you became a legend as a little boy when you almost prevented the attacks of 10/7. We *could have* avoided the attacks if those idiots at the CIA only listened to you. Well, my friend, *I'm* listening, and so is Meg. Here's the long and short of it, and it's mainly short because we don't have a lot of information. Naval Intelligence thinks there is a group of people aboard the *Ford* who plan to commit a major act of sabotage using bombs and other explosives. Leonardo, with that small bit of information I just gave you, please give us your thoughts, which I don't doubt are many."

"Yes, sir, I have some observations. The *Ford* carries an enlisted crew of 3,789, including 2,600 in the ship's company with the others in the air wing. There are 508 officers. As part of my job, I've poured through the database quite a bit. One thing that surprises me is that there is little information on most of the crew. I know that the vetting procedure for service on a carrier isn't as strict as, say, a nuclear sub, but we know little about the people with whom we serve. So, here's my recommendation, sir. As you know, my father is the Director of the Joint Terrorism Task

Force. Also, I still have some good friends in the IT department of the CIA. With your permission, sir, I would like to request that the FBI and CIA compare the *Ford's* personnel database to the FBI and CIA watch lists. A couple of phone calls and an email exchange is all it will take. People in the intelligence community have learned to listen to me, and I still have top secret clearance. Those watch lists are quite extensive. If someone on our crew shows up on either list, you will know what action to take."

"How fast can this happen?"

"The watchlist people at the CIA and FBI don't observe regular working hours. I can have our list sent to them in a couple of minutes and then they'll do the comparison checking."

"Leonardo, you're amazing."

I spoke to my dad and Buster at CIA. They both agreed to assign an agent to compare the lists. Buster said he'd do the comparing himself. Within 10 minutes I had four names of *Ford* crewmembers who are also on the intelligence watch lists. I also had their birthdates, so I was sure the suspect names were solid.

"Admiral Fenton, this is Leonardo, sir. Request permission to come to your office. You may want to ask the Chief Master at Arms to join us."

Admiral Harry, Meg, Chief Warrant Officer Dennis Ciano and I sat around the conference table in the admiral's office.

"I believe I have four suspects identified. Two of them were involved in terrorist bombings, and one of them served five years in prison. Three of the four are first class petty officers, and one is a chief petty officer. In other words, these suspects are career Navy men. If I may make a recommendation, Admiral, I suggest that some people at the Bureau of Naval Personnel should have their asses kicked."

"Dennis, arrest these bastards," Admiral Harry said. "A guy from Naval Intelligence is aboard. I suggest he join you in interrogating these sailors."

"Aye aye, sir."

"Leonardo, it's been less than an hour since I told you about the problem—and you solved it. I'm recommending you for the Distinguished Service Medal." He took out his cell phone and typed in a search string. "The Distinguished Service Medal," he read, "is awarded for 'Exceptionally meritorious service to the Government of the United States in a duty of great responsibility.' You're one hell of an officer, Leonardo."

After my promotion we put to sea for a two-week training deployment. Admiral Harry ordered me to stand watch as a junior officer of the deck and be prepared to stand watch in the future as a regular officer of the deck. Of course, he cleared it through Captain Mike Tomlinson, the commanding officer of the *Ford*. But when Admiral Harry makes a request, people know it's an order. Standing watch as an OOD is a big job, and I looked forward to it. The OOD is the direct representative of the commanding officer and has responsibility for the ship during his watch. I had already stood watch as an OOD in port on the quarterdeck, the ceremonial entrance to the ship, but Admiral Harry wanted me to stand watch underway on the bridge.

I stood my first watch as OOD two days before we returned to port. From my studies, I knew more about the *Ford* and CSG-14 than anyone, including Captain Tomlinson, Admiral Harry, and Meg. Of course, I didn't say that to anyone (only an asshole would say that). The four hours passed by quickly, and I felt great that I was now qualified as an OOD. I couldn't wait to talk to my parents about it, both of whom had stood watch as OODs.

The Navy was starting to grow on me.

Chapter 32

he shrill sound of the boatswain's pipe (or bosun's pipe) sounded throughout the *Ford* and the other three ships in Carrier Strike Group 14. For some crazy reason, I've gotten to love the sound of the pipe. As my mom would say, it sounds "salty."

"Attention all hands, attention all hands, stand by for Admiral Harry Fenton."

"Good afternoon, everybody," Admiral Fenton said. "I've just received word from Naval Operations that our strike group will deploy overseas in four days. I know that's extremely short notice for you and your families, but I assure you that NavOps wouldn't give such an order without good reason. As Navy Regs require with such a sudden announcement, I can't tell you now just where we'll be headed. Once we're underway you will know more as the days go by. All I can tell you is that our mission may be dangerous. That is all. Carry on."

After his announcement, Admiral Harry called a meeting of his "executive committee," Meg and me.

"So, tell me, my cryptic hubby, are you going to share your little secret with Leonardo and me?"

"I thought you'd never ask. So, here's the deal. You may want to sip some water first. What I'm about to tell you might be scary. Leonardo, tell us what you know about Concordia."

"Holy shit," Meg said.

"Somehow I knew you'd say that," Admiral Harry said.

"Well, sir, the CIA asked me to do some research for them about three years ago, shortly after Concordia split off from Santa Mallarta. As we know, Concordia is a small nation which took power from Santa Mallarta after their president died and left the country's economy in shambles. What confuses everybody, including the American government, is where Concordia gets its resources. They seem to be drowning in money, and nobody knows where it comes from. What the new government didn't have, God knows, was much oil revenue because of the idiotic economic programs the former leader put in play. That may be changing, at least since the last time I studied the issue. A shocker is that Concordia has been building a substantial navy, although they don't have an aircraft carrier—yet."

"Leonardo, our orders are to steam close to the main Concordian fleet and see if we can detect any hostile intent. NavOps gave me the location of the ships. Leonardo, I want you to wrap that brain of yours around Concordia and update the research you did three years ago. We have super-fast Internet service on the *Ford*, so you will have plenty to sort through. I'm not able to give you a question to work on, just a general directive to find out anything you possibly can about this pipsqueak nation."

"From your announcement, sir, I understand that we go to sea in four days. I think I can have a pile of information for you by the day before we set sail."

"Don't hesitate to bounce your thoughts off my lovely chief of staff here. Before I met you, Meg was one of the smartest people I ever encountered."

"What do you mean '*one* of the smartest'?" Meg asked.

"Gimme a kiss, wiseass."

Working with the Fentons is one of life's pleasures.

The day before we were due to deploy, I told Meg that my report was finished. She was invaluable in helping me with the research. At 12:15, Admiral Harry walked into his dining room on the flag bridge. To save time, Meg ordered lunch to be served to us.

"Meg tells me that you two have come up with some startling information."

"Startling is the word, Admiral. First, I'd like to say that I've collaborated with some sharp people in my life, especially at Harvard, but few as smart as Lieutenant Meg here." I wasn't just throwing out a compliment. I meant it.

"Yes, Leonardo, I married well. So, what have you got for me?"

Meg handed Admiral Harry two documents, a 95-page report that I prepared and a 10-page summary report that Meg had put together for this meeting. She is brilliant at synthesizing a long report for easy discussion.

"Bottom line, Admiral, is that Concordia has assembled a sizeable navy with modern ships. Her fleet today stands at 100 ships, a lot bigger than you'd expect for such a small country. The only assets she dfive fairly new diesel subs. Concordia has 30 frigates, 15 guided missile cruisers, 30 destroyers, and 15 fast gunboats. They've recruited officers and sailors across the world, including Russians, Iranians, and North Koreans."

"Can you give me an opinion of their intentions?"

Meg put her face in her hands when the admiral asked that question.

"I can't believe I'm saying this, sir, but Concordia is gunning for us."

Chapter 33

eonardo, Meg, do you realize what you're saying? A little piss-ant nation with a bunch of ships would dare attack the United States Navy? What would their goal be, besides suicide?"

"Admiral, besides being pretty good at research, I also know how to hack computers and websites, which is illegal, but so what, I did it. As you know I'm fluent in Spanish and all the Spanish dialects of Latin America. A lot of quotations are in the longer report but let me just summarize by saying that Concordia plans to become a major power by crippling the world's shipping industry. One of its methods will be to attack US Navy ships to keep us off balance so Concordia can go about sinking private ships, including cruise ships."

"Leonardo, do we know who the players are? Is it the current administration of Concordia? Is one nut running this show?"

"Yes, sir, amazing as it is to say it, there appears to be one man at the head of their operations and strategy. Here's the strange part: Not once did we see his name, or even his initials. He is generally referred to as 'Him,' or 'Our Friend,' or simply, 'The Man,' always capitalized. I've never seen anything like this, nor could I have imagined it."

"Meg?" Admiral Harry said as he looked at her. They were having one of their one-word communications.

"I completely agree with Leonardo, Harry. One guy is running this show."

"Okay," Admiral Harry said. "I need some time to digest this stuff. I want to read through Leonardo's long report. I can't believe you put this together in three days. You two are the only staff I need. Let me be alone for a little while. I'll be calling you both with questions."

"Aren't you supposed to say, 'that is all, carry on,' honey?"

"Meg, you'll always be my favorite wiseass."

Chapter 34

Two days after we put to sea I stood watch on the bridge as OOD. It was 0500, five in the morning.

"Lieutenant Murphy," said the Ensign Joe Fleming, the JOOD, "radar reports a group of ten ships steaming over the horizon. They're cruising in formation, sir."

Cruising in formation? Probably a naval flotilla.

"What's their heading, Joe?"

"Three six zero, sir. They're aiming straight at us."

"Call the captain and the admiral. I'm sounding general quarters."

The general quarters command means that all hands must report to their battle stations immediately. Normally I would alert the captain before sounding the general quarters alarm, but there wasn't enough time. I alerted the OODs on the other ships in our group.

"General quarters, general quarters," I yelled into the microphone, accompanied by the jarring sound of a claxon, "all hands man your battle stations. This is not a drill. I repeat, this is not a drill."

Captain Tomlinson appeared on the bridge, followed by Admiral Harry and Meg.

"I'll take it, Lieutenant," the captain said.

Tomlinson poked his head into the pilot house and announced, "This is Captain Tomlinson, I have the con," telling the helmsman and others that he had control of the ship. It's customary, during general quarters, for the captain to take command. I was relieved to be relieved.

He then ordered a fly-over of six drones to show us what the flotilla looked like. He and Admiral Harry poured over the photos as they showed up on a monitor.

"Those ships are from Concordia," the captain said. "They look exactly like the other ships we've spotted."

"As I told you, Mike, Lieutenant Murphy's research tells us that Concordia has some heavy firepower," Admiral Harry said. "We're looking at four frigates and six destroyers."

Meg pulled me aside by the sleeve. "Hey, Leonardo, now isn't the time for humility. Tell Harry exactly what you're thinking."

"Admiral Fenton, may I make a recommendation, sir?"

"Go ahead, Leonardo."

"We have aboard a visiting officer from the Colombian Navy. I suggest that you order him to the bridge to observe what may happen. If we need to fire on the Concordian flotilla, he will be a witness for you when Concordia raises hell at the UN."

"Good idea. You call him. His English is a bit weak and you speak Spanish."

As Commander Portillo entered the bridge, we could see the masts of the leading Concordian ships on the horizon.

"Leonardo, come over here and look at the monitor," Admiral Harry said. "We have a good aerial view of the Concordian ships. From your research, does anything jump out at you?"

"Yes, sir, all of the ships carry extra missile launch platforms. They're prepared for battle."

"Incoming!" the JOOD shouted, "two missiles off the starboard bow."

All of the ships in CSG-14 are equipped with the Aegis missile defense system, an amazing piece of technology that enables a ship to shoot down a fast-approaching missile. Both missiles were aimed at the *Ford*. The Aegis radar intercepted them, but a large piece of a rocket flew through the window. The captain had ordered the window left open so we could have a clear view even though we were at general quarters. The object crashed into an overhead pipe, which fell right toward Admiral Harry. Using my gentle judo I studied as a kid, I wrapped my arms around the admiral and flipped him to the deck.

"God bless you, pal. God bless you," Admiral Harry said as we picked ourselves off the deck.

"Air Ops, this is the bridge. Prepare to launch aircraft," the captain said to Air Operations. "Are you there, Bill?" he said to the "air boss," Commander Bill Romaine.

"I'm here, Captain. Do you want me to launch Hornets?"

He was referring to F/A-18 Super Hornets, some of the most sophisticated and deadly fighters in the fleet—and Meg's favorite as well as mine.

"Yes, prepare to launch eight Hornets."

Meg looked at Admiral Harry, about to engage in one of their wordless conversations.

"Don't even think about it, babe. I need my chief of staff right here." Admiral Harry obviously had no intention of letting her fly into harm's way.

Our eight Hornets circled a safe distance from the Concordian flotilla.

"Leonardo," Admiral Harry said, "you predicted that Concordia is gunning for us, and as usual you were right. Don't be shy. What would you do if you were me?"

I couldn't believe an admiral was asking me for tactical advice.

"Sir, we have the capability of taking out that entire flotilla, but I would recommend that we only attack the frigate that fired on us. That will make the Concordian admiral rethink his ideas."

Captain Tomlinson was listening to our conversation.

"I concur with Lieutenant Murphy. Let's take out that frigate and see if they decide to stand down."

The words *stand down* always amazed me. How the hell do you stand *down*? Don't you stand *up*? My brain sometimes goes in its own direction whether I want it to or not.

We opened fire on the Concordian frigate with missiles from one of our destroyers, and bombs and more missiles from our circling Hornets. Within minutes, the ship capsized and sank.

We heard a man's voice shouting over our radio in Spanish. He claimed that the missiles fired at us were a mistake and requested that we cease fire.

"Leonardo, tell him we're standing down and order him to do the same. Tell him to proceed on his current course."

I did as Admiral Harry ordered, and the guy thanked me profusely. Obviously, we did more than call their bluff.

The flotilla continued on its heading, showing no further signs of hostile intent. The Concordian admiral wisely concluded, after losing one ship, that his flotilla was no match for our strike group.

The incident passed, and Admiral Harry allowed the Concordian flotilla to proceed on its way.

After an hour, Captain Tomlinson gave the con back to me. On his order, I announced that we were securing from battle stations.

So, our little crisis was over. But from what I researched, I knew that our dealings with Concordia would never be friendly.

Chapter 35

After four years in the Navy, I mustered out with the rank of full lieutenant. Meg Fenton was promoted to lieutenant commander shortly after I became a lieutenant. As I had expected, my time in the Navy was exciting. I was involved in a naval battle, one of the scarier experiences of my life. And getting my pilot's wings and qualifying on an F/A-18 Super Hornet can only be described as peak experiences.

I'll never forget serving with Harry and Meg Fenton. Those two are so close they complete each other's sentences and speak without speaking. I hoped I'd meet a woman someday who I could be that close to.

I returned to New York and to my condo, which I rented out during my time in the Navy. I'm only 24, and I've got lots of ideas. What else is new?

I'm still close as ever to my folks. Although I visited them during my Navy years, they wanted to hear everything about my service, especially about flying jets. We rented a nice cottage in East Hampton and spent a great weekend talking about my Navy—and theirs. I recalled that, when Mom heard about my Distinguished Service Medal, she went absolutely batshit. She flipped out again when I was awarded the Silver Star for gallantry for saving Admiral Harry's life (and risking my own) when we were attacked by the rocket. They were blown away by my story of how I was engaged in a naval battle.

A month ago they invited me to have dinner with them and their friends, the Bellamys. Ellen, the former love of my young life, is still topping the ratings with *The Ellen Bellamy Show*, which had become an American institution. Ellen invited her younger sister, Janice Reynolds, to join us. Ellen made sure that Janice and I sat next to each other. I felt like I just launched off a carrier deck. Oh my God, what a beautiful lady. She could be Ellen's twin although she was my age. Janice is tall, about 5'10", four inches shorter than me, with natural blond hair like her sister. Also, like her sister, Janice has beautiful blue eyes, from which I had a hard time averting mine. After a few minutes I stopped trying, and just stared into those beautiful eyes. Her perfume smelled like Ellen's. The conversation around the table was fun and animated, but I don't recall hearing anyone else besides Janice. I regaled her with my exciting days in the Navy, but I have no idea what I said. Janice has a way of making a point that I found wonderful. She would grab my hand when she wanted to say something important. Once, after telling me a funny story, we kept holding hands. It just felt natural as if we'd been together for years.

At the end of the evening as we all stood in front of the restaurant waiting for cabs, I asked Janice if she would like to go to a show—the next night. She put her face close to mine and said softly, "That would be really nice." No big deal. A simple sentence signaling approval. But for some reason I'll never forget it. Janice thought it would be nice to see me again.

Janice and I dated constantly since that night—as if we didn't want to be apart. I guess we didn't. After our third date, I realized that I was in love and shared my feelings with Janice. She told me the same. She has a way of saying the nicest things to me. "When I first saw you as a scrawny little nerd on my sister's show a few years ago, I thought you were kind of cute, in a propeller-head sort of way." She said. "Well, now you're a grown-up nerd—and handsome as hell. Ellen told me that you had a big crush on her for years."

"How did she know that?" I said.

"Ellen said that you constantly sent her flowers and gushing emails. You may have been a little nerd, but you were a romantic little nerd. I'm glad to see that you're still romantic—and not in love with my big sister anymore."

"Do you realize this is our third date?" I asked. "It seems like I've known you forever."

"I thought this was our second," she said.

"I'm counting the dinner with my folks and the Bellamys as our first. So, this is our third date."

She put her hands on my chest and stared into my eyes. "Well in that case we're not rushing anything if we go back to my place—or yours."

Janice does not suffer from shyness.

Janice isn't just a lover, she's a good friend, probably my best friend. Like Ellen, Janice is smart. She graduated from Brown University number one in her class. She was an English literature major, which I thought was great. I get bored talking about physics and computer science all the time. She's been helping me with my Jane Austen program, filling me in with her vast knowledge of English literature. Austen has now written 10 novels, two of which became best sellers. Janice confessed once that she's intimidated by my oversized brain, but I make sure she has no reason to feel that way. Yes, grandpa, don't be an asshole, especially around a great woman like Janice Reynolds. I've noticed that, when Janice and I are talking, she would often look at me and say nothing, but I got her communication just from her look. Our relationship started to remind me of Admiral Harry and Meg.

Like Grandpa Ezekiel, I've gotten a few patents, 71 to be exact. Most of them are in computer science, although one of my favorites is a lawn mower that doesn't cut grass with blades, but with high frequency sound waves. Cool—and safe. I invented the mower after I read about a little kid getting his foot cut off by lawnmower blades.

With all my projects and patents, not to mention my stock trading talents, I'm kind of loaded, quite wealthy in fact. Admiral Harry once joked, after he read an article about my investing, that I could buy the *Ford*.

I sold my condo and bought a brownstone building near my parents' apartment in Manhattan. It's on Fifth Avenue and 66th Street, with a great view of Central Park. Janice helped me pick it out and she loves it. The front door, painted red, is the classic Manhattan brownstone entrance. The house is huge, with four floors, eight bedrooms, and 12 bathrooms. The kitchen is so large it could be used for catering. Our favorite room is the den, which measures 25 by 35 feet. It has a large window overlooking Fifth Avenue and the park. I was still readjusting myself from living in a cramped stateroom on the Ford.

We were planning to get married next year when we'll both be 25, still young but who cares. Even with my crazy imagination, I can't imagine life without Janice, so why not make it forever? We didn't make a public announcement yet, but we were engaged.

I took a selfie of us and emailed it to Admiral Harry and Meg.

The email I got back, over both their names, said. "Leave it to Leonardo Murphy to do his research and find a wonderful woman like Janice Reynolds." I miss those two.

Chapter 36

anice's birthday was three months away and I wanted to surprise her. One of the few projects I hadn't tackled was painting. If Leonardo da Vinci was known as one of the great painters of all time, I shouldn't have his name if I didn't start to paint.

Like I do with most of my projects, I decided to go all in. I enrolled in an art class at Columbia University. I knew one of the professors there from a course I took at Harvard. Max Lieboldt is a talented painter and specializes in landscapes. His favorite school of art is the Hudson River School, which is also my favorite. Many of his works hang in the lobbies of major corporations. He's also a great teacher. I enrolled in his course on oil painting.

The painting I wanted to do was firmly in my mind. I could see it as if it already existed. It would be a scene from my childhood. My parents once took me to a beautiful inn in the Catskills. The view from our porch is indelibly printed on my brain. It's as if I could close my eyes and look at it, which I did. The scene was a mountain valley lined with treed hills on each side. A lake shimmered in the distance, and the early fall foliage is with me to this day.

I don't like to skimp on projects, and I can afford to spend money on my whims. The top floor of our house in Manhattan is a finished attic. I had a large picture window installed as well as a skylight to let in natural light. The attic became my studio.

I convinced Janice not to go to the attic until I was done with my painting. Of course, I didn't tell her it was a painting, just that it was something I wanted to dedicate to her.

As I always do with a new project, I completely immersed myself. After a month of art lessons, I felt confident that I could paint the scene that was in my mind. Professor Max, although not one given to easy praise, freaked out over my work. "I won't bullshit you, Leonardo," Max said. "I have never seen a student progress so fast. I don't like to exaggerate, so I won't. Your work is beautiful, as good as I've ever seen."

Professor Max knew how to encourage a student.

For my gift to Janice, I chose a large canvas, four by six feet. I'll never forget when I began the painting. Stephen King, discussing novels, says that stories are like fossils. They already exist, and the novelist's job is to unearth them and show them to the world. I believe the same applies to art, especially a painting. The painting was already there—in my mind. I just used the techniques I learned in class to bring what was already there to life. I worked on the painting four hours a day for three weeks. Although I'm 6'2" I needed to climb onto a bench to put my paint strokes on the upper parts of the canvas.

I wanted to present Janice with my best work possible, so I invited Professor Max to give me his honest critique before I sprung it on her. The painting was just about done.

Max wept, he actually wept.

"Leonardo, I think you should change your last name as well. DaVinci has a nice sound to it," Max said as he blew his nose.

Janice's birthday present was almost ready. I decided to add something to the painting. In the foreground, walking up through the valley, I painted Janice with that beautiful smile on her face.

Her 25nd birthday arrived on a Saturday. I ordered a catered breakfast to start the day right.

"So, when do I get to see the big surprise you've been keeping from me, Lee?"

Janice is the only person in the world who I allow to call me anything but Leonardo. Well, her and my old FBI pal Gladys Jackson, who called me Lombardo.

"The time has come," I said. I took her by the hand and we walked up to my studio. Every now and then I have a flair for the dramatic. So, I had covered the painting with a sheet. It took me some practice the day before to yank one string and have the sheet fall to the floor. I yanked. The sheet fell.

Janice was silent. She walked up to the painting, then took a couple of steps backward. Five minutes passed without her saying a word. I was getting nervous. Finally, she spoke.

"Oh, my God, Lee. You did this—for me? And that girl in the painting, it's me!"

"So, you like it?"

"Like it? I feel like I've passed through to another reality. It's the most beautiful painting I've ever seen, and I'm not saying that to flatter you. It's brilliant, Lee, it's astonishing."

She sat on a bench. "Come, sit next to me, Lee. I don't want to take my eyes off the painting. I want to imprint it on my mind so it never leaves me."

Chapter 37

Janice was teaching English literature at Champlin College, a new private school on 86th Street. I love to see a person who loves her job. Every evening she would tell me stories about her students and the things they accomplished. When she talked about her students, her face lit up like a sunflower. She told me about each of the kids in such detail I felt as though I knew them. God, she so totally cares about other people. I was worried, however, because I kept seeing articles in the newspaper about the financial problems the college was going through. It seems that the administration played hooky from the course on managing finances. They ran the place like a grocery store.

A week before the end of the semester, Janice came into the house crying. I had no idea what the problem was, so I simply said her name. It's a way of communicating I learned from Harry and Meg Fenton.

"Hey, Lee, gimme a kiss. Let's go to the den and sit in front of your painting. It calms me down and reminds me of the good in the world. Because what I have to tell you isn't good—it sucks."

"Talk to me, honey."

"They just announced that Champlin College is closing—immediately," she said, blowing her nose. "The poor kids who were supposed to graduate next month are not going to. Lee, you should have given those jerks who ran the place a quick course on financial management. I'm sorry I'm being so emotional, honey, but I really loved teaching there."

"Hey, it makes me upset to see you upset. Gimme another kiss."

"Thanks, baby, that always makes me feel better."

"I have a few ideas."

"Leonardo Murphy has a *few ideas*? Like the Atlantic Ocean has a few fish?"

"Let's talk about what we can do," I said. "Hell, I've read that Champlin College has one of the highest rated academic programs in the state, even though it's only been around for a few years. It can't just close."

"I wish I could agree that it can't close, but it *is* closing, Lee. The president, Nat Rimland, announced it this morning. It will be on the news tonight."

She started crying again.

"Didn't you tell me that you're friends with Rimland?"

"Yes, we are friends. He's a good guy and had little to do with this crap. Although a college president is supposed to control a school's finances, the board of trustees insisted on total fiscal governance. I think the only requirement to serve on the board is that you have to be an idiot. Nat Rimland would often confide to me over coffee that he was worried about the money. He told me that Champlin is $25 million in debt. Hey, hon, I can hear the synapses in your brain firing. What are you thinking?"

"I think I'll buy the school."

"Buy the school? Are you serious? Hey, Lee, I never asked you, but how much money *do* you have anyway?"

"Just shy of 35," I said.

"Thirty-five what?"

"Thirty-five bil, and it keeps growing."

"By bil do you mean *billion* with a 'b'? Like 35 billion friggin dollars?"

"Yeah, and it's not just mine, it's *our* money."

Janice just stared at me. She knew I had a few bucks, but she was kind of amazed that I had *that* much. My patent royalties and stock trading have paid off over the past few years.

"My God, honey, you're serious, aren't you?"

"I can easily pay off the $25 million debt and fund a large endowment. Why don't you call Rimland and tell him not to make a public announcement about the school closing? Call him right now."

"Champlin College, may I help you?

"Hi Doris, it's Janice Reynolds. Can I speak to Dr. Rimland please?"

"He's in a meeting as I'm sure you can understand, Janice. I think he's planning the big announcement."

"Doris, please interrupt the meeting. It's urgent that I speak to him."

"I think he'll be furious, even though he's fond of you. Can I tell him what it's about?"

"Just tell him that he doesn't need to make the announcement. I have good news for him."

"Hi, Janice, Nat Rimland here. Doris says you need to speak to me about something urgent, and that it's also good news. My heart is pounding, so why don't you tell me the good news."

"Champlin College has an angel investor."

"Oh my God. Who is it?"

"None other than my fiancé, Leonardo Murphy. He wants to say hello."

"Hello, Dr. Rimland, Leonardo Murphy here."

"Please the name is Nat. May I call you Leonardo?"

"Of course. Your problems are over, at least financially. I'm going to buy the college. Janice has told me all about your board of directors who didn't do much directing. She tells me that you have no fiscal control at all and that your board controlled all the finances. I would like you to stay on as president. The clowns on the board will have to go, of course. I'm going to round up my advisors and we'll meet with you at the college tomorrow. If any reporters call you, I suggest you tell the truth, that a last-minute investor has come forward. That should avoid your creditors hitting the panic button. I'll see you tomorrow at 10 in the morning."

"Lee," Janice said as she wrapped her arms around me, "I love you. Oh my God do I love you."

Chapter 38

The next day I met with Nat Rimland, president of Champlin. Janice was with me, of course, as well as Jerry Blankfein, my financial advisor, Sam Thurgood, senior partner at my accounting firm, and Frank Randazzo, my attorney.

"Dr. Rimland," Frank Randazzo said, "My client isn't prepared to make a firm offer of course, because we need to go through due diligence of the school's finances and all other matters. But Mr. Murphy is prepared to act immediately when we're done and have agreed on a price. Because the school is insolvent, the price offer may be limited to paying off the $25 million debt, and the equity in the building."

Due diligence is the process where a purchaser looks into every nook and cranny of a seller's business. We expected to find a lot of financial mistakes. What we didn't expect was criminal activity, but that's exactly what we found. The trustees not only neglected the books, they raided them, pocketing millions. Frank Randazzo contacted the Manhattan DA, and indictments started to flow. Two of the trustees fled to places unknown. As we expected, Nat Rimland, who was not on the board, was clean of any wrongdoing. He's the only hero in this mess, having turned Champlin into an outstanding academic institution. All the creditors were contacted and agreed to wait for the results of our due diligence before making any moves to collect. I deposited $50 million into escrow and that made the creditors relax a bit, knowing that they had a good chance of being paid off. Although the college is private, I intend to run it as a nonprofit and invest any profits (really just income over expenses) into the general endowment. I also intend to contribute an additional $10 million to a scholarship fund for bright but financially needy kids.

Neither Janice nor I wanted to be involved in the complications of running an institution, so I carefully picked a board of talented trustees. Janice was happy to continue teaching.

I gave an immediate contribution to the school so that it could continue while all the legal and financial details were ironed out. I wanted to make sure that Janice's students would have the graduation they deserved.

But I had other ideas for Janice.

Chapter 39

 can't believe you just bought a college, Lee. Being around you is never boring."

"Besides teaching college, what do you love to do?"

"Make love to you."

"God, you have a wonderful way of saying things. But besides that, what else?"

"You know. I love to write. When I'm writing a novel, I tune out the world, just like you told me you did with your beautiful painting. When I'm writing a novel, it's like opening a door and walking into a new universe. I lose myself in my characters and the story, and the novel unfolds in front of me. It's almost as if my characters are showing me the story and I'm just writing it down. But hey, my handsome fiancé has come up with a computer program that writes novels. That intimidates the hell out of me, Lee. I mean, good grief, your Austen program can crank out a finished book in a couple of hours. That makes me feel insecure."

"Austen can never compete with you, baby. The only reason I keep playing around with the program is to test the outer limits of artificial intelligence. Wanna know the difference between what Austen writes and what you write?"

"Yeah, Austen writes a lot faster than me."

"No, that's not the difference. Passion, that's the difference—passion. Sure, I can load Austen's brain with zillions of words and rules, but what you write grabs me by the heart, not just my head. It's passion, honey, of which you've got plenty. Your last novel, *The Johnson Dilemma*, brought me to tears every time I opened it."

"Hey, Lee, what do you mean every time you opened it? You read a 500-page book in 20 minutes."

"I kept opening it because I read it five times in one night. I can never get enough of a good thing—like one of your novels."

"So, what's your big idea, honey? I mean *one* of your big ideas."

"Why don't you write full time? I know you like teaching at the college we now own, but expand your thinking. Be the great novelist that you already are and share your creative brain with the world. And with my newfound art skills I can create terrific book covers."

Janice put her arms around me. She was crying, but I don't think she was unhappy. I think she likes my idea of her writing full time. Janice always cries when she feels strong emotions, including happiness.

"The only thing I don't like about writing is pitching agents and going through those disgusting rejection letters, Lee. I'll never forget a rejection I got 30 seconds after I sent the damn manuscript by email. The agent said that she enjoyed my manuscript very much and noted that I had obvious talent, but

I was not the right fit for her at that time. I mean, Lee, even you can't read and evaluate a friggin manuscript in 30 seconds."

"So, let's talk about you self-publishing—in style. Some of the best writers out there are self-published. I can hire the best editors money can buy. We can set up our own publishing company."

"Lee, honey, you find it impossible to think small about anything don't you?"

"Hey, I launched a satellite into space when I was 12 years old. Why stop now?"

Chapter 40

"Tick, tick, tick, tick, tick, tick, tick, tick, tick."

ood evening, ladies and gentleman. I'm Steve Croft for *60 Minutes*. Tonight's show will consist of one segment, a story about a young man who is probably the smartest person in the country, if not the world. I'm speaking, of course, about Leonardo Murphy, a 25-year old-man with the second highest IQ ever recorded. We're taping from Leonardo's beautiful brownstone building in Manhattan. You'll see why we chose this location shortly, but first I want to introduce you to a guy who makes me feel like a high school dropout. Leonardo—nobody calls him Leo—was first introduced to the public 13 years ago by our CBS colleague Ellen Bellamy on *The Ellen Bellamy Show*. He was 12 years old at the time, and became an instant celebrity, although you'd never know it. Leonardo has a reputation as a gentleman, a just plain regular guy. Leonardo is now engaged to Janice Reynolds, the younger sister of Ellen Bellamy, who takes deserved credit for introducing them. He may be smarter than the rest of us, but you'd never know it from his outgoing personality. Ask him a few questions, as Ellen did on that famous show, and you quickly realize why he's called Leonardo, a name he personally chose and formally adopted because he wanted to honor his hero, Leonardo da Vinci. We may think of Leonardo da Vinci as the Leonardo Murphy of the 15th Century. Leonardo currently owns 71 patents on everything from computer algorithms to a bladeless lawnmower. Besides his income from patent royalties, he makes a fortune

every year from trading stocks and commodities, a talent he picked up after reading a couple of books on investing when he was 10 years old. Like his namesake, Leonardo da Vinci, Mr. Murphy is a polymath, a person with-ranging knowledge of a multitude of subjects.

"He's also an unabashed patriot. After graduating from Harvard with a PhD in physics, the world was his oyster. So, what did Leonardo do? He joined the Navy to follow in his parents' footsteps as a naval officer. He left the service after four years with the rank of lieutenant. He also holds the wings of a naval aviator. The famous Admiral Harry Fenton, on whose staff Leonardo served, awarded him the Distinguished Service Medal for some amazing intelligence work Leonardo did. Although the circumstances are top secret, we've been told that Leonardo's efforts on the *USS Gerald R. Ford* avoided what could have been a major naval disaster. He also risked his life when he saved Admiral Fenton from being struck by a pipe that was hit by a missile. That action won him the Silver Star for gallantry.

"Leonardo, it's a pleasure and an honor to have you with us on *60 Minutes*."

"The honor's all mine, Steve."

"I was going to ask you to tell us a bit about yourself, but our segment would need to be a couple of months long for you to answer. So, let me ask you some specific questions. When did you learn your first foreign language?"

"I started when I was four. By the time I was five, I was fluent in Chinese Mandarin, French, German, Italian, Japanese, Portuguese, Russian, and Spanish. A few years ago, I learned Arabic."

"This may be a difficult question to answer, but when did you realize that you were different?"

"My parents told me—constantly. My dad is an FBI agent and is now Director of the Joint Terrorism Task Force, and Mom is the Chief Homicide Detective with the NYPD. I would overhear them talking shop and I'd often help them with their cases. On a few occasions I even solved the case. That started when I was around seven."

"Leonardo, you're a grown man now, although still young. When people hear about your early achievements they assume that you were probably a spoiled brat. Care to comment on that?"

"Yes, I had all the potential to be an obnoxious brat, but my great grandfather stopped that from happening."

"How did he do that?"

"Grandpa Ezekiel was a brilliant man himself. He held over 300 patents. He saw that I inherited his brains and warned me in a way I'll never forget. Your sound engineer may want to bleep out what I'm about to say, but for you to get it, I'll have to say it. 'Leonardo,' grandpa said, 'whatever you do—don't be an asshole.'"

Croft cracked up.

"If we bleep that out we'd lose grandpa's intention," he said.

"Those words have stuck with me and I try my best to obey them."

"When the CIA and FBI heard you would be our guest, they carefully vetted the *60 Minutes* crew on certain secret matters that we can't discuss. But there is one matter you worked on as a young consultant to the CIA that has been made public, so we will talk about it. You, Leonardo Murphy, almost prevented the horrors of 10/7. We've interviewed dozens of agents with the FBI and CIA, and they all confirmed that the people in charge of intelligence gathering simply chose to ignore your warnings about the timing of the attacks. Would you care to comment on that?"

"Yes, and I still get furious when I think about the attacks, even though they were 12 years ago. I was 13 years old at the time, and yes, I had been hired as a paid consultant to the CIA. As you've been told, I designed a computer algorithm to track down suspected terrorists. I kept warning anyone who would listen, and a lot of people did, including my dad, that I couldn't be certain about the timing of the attacks. I tried to convince the powers-that-be to simply arrest the suspects and avoid disaster. But no, the man in charge wanted to exercise patience. The result of his ignoring my warnings was 10/7."

"Leonardo, can we please move into the den? As prearranged, we have with us Dr. Jason Snyder, curator of The National Gallery of Art, and generally recognized as one of the nation's foremost experts on oil painting."

Croft had arranged with me to do the honors of taking down the sheet covering my painting. I pulled the string, and Janice's birthday present came into view. Janice was there with us.

Dr. Snyder walked up to the painting, then stepped back.

"Oh, my God," he said. "I don't want to spoil this moment with a lot of words. Let me just say that this is one of the finest oil paintings I've ever seen. It's breathtaking."

He then pointed to various spots on the painting and commented on the brush strokes and other techniques I used.

Steve Croft had insisted that he didn't want to see the painting until the segment aired. He wanted to show the audience his real emotions. He was uncharacteristically speechless. He then walked over to Janice.

"Janice, that's you in the painting, isn't it?"

"Yes, Steve. Can you possibly imagine a nicer birthday present?"

"No, I can't, Janice. No, I can't."

A tear rolled down his cheek.

The image panned back to the CBS Studio.

"This is Lesley Stahl, signing off for my speechless colleague, Steve Croft. Please join us next week for another segment of *60 Minutes*."

Although the show was taped and could have been edited, the producers chose to leave in the scene of Steve Croft crying over the painting.

Chapter 41

he night after my *60 Minutes* taping, I took Janice to a nice little restaurant we both love. It's a small place with only 10 tables. The wait staff seems dedicated to making people relax. Janice was getting excited about the idea of writing full time. I wasn't kidding her when I said I love her work—and I didn't say that just to make her happy.

Typical me, I was prattling on and on about the structure of our soon-to-be-formed publishing company. Having had a few of my books published I was kind of familiar with the publishing business. I talked about hiring great editors and production people, and even spoke about a building for sale on Madison Avenue, a perfect spot for a publishing house.

"Honey," she said, "setting up a publishing company like you're talking about takes a lot of effort and money. God knows you have the money, but do you really want those headaches? The competition is fierce, and you have to deal with the likes of Amazon."

"I want you to be the great novelist that you are. You create new worlds, and your fiction enriches people's lives. Our money will enable you to keep doing it. I want to paint a picture of you typing at your keyboard."

"Have I mentioned how much I love you, Lee?"

"Hey, on that very subject, let's formally announce our engagement. We've been talking about it, but I think it's time to set a date. I want to be with you forever."

Chapter 42

Good afternoon, ladies and gentlemen, and welcome to *The Ellen Bellamy Show*. Although I don't usually announce news features, I have the privilege of breaking an important story. Janice Reynolds, my little sister—well, she's not little anymore—has just announced her engagement to a wonderful man you all know, Leonardo Murphy. You may recall a few years ago when little 12-year-old Leonardo was a guest on my show talking about a few of his amazing inventions and projects. Leonardo became a household name a few short years ago because of his prodigious talents. He is known to have the second highest IQ ever recorded. Leonardo used to be a cute little nerd, but now he's a 25-year-old extremely handsome nerd, as my sister loves to say. And his amazing mind is showing no sign of slowing down, as he's awarded patent after patent. I must take a little credit for these terrific people getting married. Just a year ago, my husband and I went to dinner with our good friends, Jack and Rebecca Murphy. I suggested they invite their son Leonardo to join us, and I secretly invited Janice to be there. So just call me Ellen the Yenta. I couldn't be happier for my little sister. Leonardo Murphy, with a brain the size of Texas, is a polite and unassuming gentleman, a plain nice guy. They will marry next month. I've been asked to keep the location private, so I will.

"And now for my first guest…"

Chapter 43

e got married at St. Mark's Episcopal Church near our house in Manhattan. Most of the people we invited were friends of Janice. I hate to say it, but my years at Harvard were kind of insular because I worked on most of my projects alone. Although I hated my CIA experience, I did make a couple of good friends, so Jim Locklear and Buster were at our wedding. Gladys Jackson was there, my FBI pal from the safe house in Connecticut. The note with her wedding present—two tickets to the New York Philharmonic—said, "Dear *Lombardo*. Make beautiful music with your beautiful bride." Gladys hasn't stopped being cool.

We invited Admiral Harry Fenton and his wife, Lieutenant Commander Meg. I was blown away when they accepted, but they had to cancel because Admiral Harry's strike group was deployed to a hot spot a week before the wedding.

Janice's parents, Bob and Melinda Reynolds, are great people, as I'd expect for folks who raised Janice. They sat with my mom and dad. My parents were so happy I thought they'd fall over. Ellen Bellamy kept her promise and didn't disclose the date or place of our wedding on her show. Ellen was Janice's maid of honor and Rick Bellamy was my best man.

The priest who married us was Father Rick Sampson, formerly Navy Commander Sampson, Chaplain of the *USS Gerald R. Ford* when I was stationed on the ship. He looked me up when he became pastor of St. Mark's, and I told him immediately that I wanted him to join us in marriage.

We picked the Four Seasons for our reception. Janice's parents wanted to pay for it as the traditional gesture of giving the bride away, but I flatly refused. They make nice incomes as two financial executives, but I'm loaded, and I didn't think it was appropriate. They insisted that I take the money—$80,000—and donate it to a charity of my choice. I picked the Navy-Marine Corps Relief Society, a foundation that provides all sorts of assistance, financial and otherwise, to sailors and Marines. I suggested that they make the donation directly so they could get the tax write-off.

Janice composed and recited a beautiful poem. It was a surprise. The poem ended with the words, "...and he's mine, for ever and ever." I don't like to cry in public, but I broke down. Then *I* had a surprise. I don't have a great singing voice, but I play a pretty good guitar. I sang "Here Comes the Sun," my favorite Beatles song. When I think of Janice, I think of a beautiful sunrise.

We were booked on the *Queen Mary 2* for our honeymoon three days after the wedding.

Little did I know that I would get a big surprise the day before our cruise.

Chapter 44

ee, honey, your dad's on the phone."

"Hi Dad, how's everything? Let's plan on getting together for dinner when Janice and I get back from our cruise."

"Sounds great. Hey, Leonardo, there's a man in my office who would like to talk to you."

"Sure, put him on."

"Well, he'd like to meet you here, if that works for you."

"Can you give me a hint what it's about? I hope he's not one of your old spy friends."

"No, he's not, but he does request privacy."

"I'll be there in a half hour."

As a top FBI honcho, dad loves secrecy. I guess it gets into your blood. I was curious as hell who this guy was.

"Your father's in his office, Leonardo. Just go ahead in," his assistant said.

Sitting across from my father at a conference table was a man who looked familiar. He was about six feet, had gray hair, and reading glasses perched on the end of his nose. Hey, I thought, I know who this guy is—Thomas Bixby, President Morton's chief of staff.

"Leonardo, meet my old friend Tom Bixby. I'm sure you recognize him from his many television appearances."

"Sure, you're President Morton's chief of staff. Pleasure to meet you, sir."

Why the heck is the president's right-hand man talking to me? I'd find out soon enough, I figured. After some preliminary chit chat, Bixby, an imposing, structured, square-jawed man looked into my eyes. I had heard this about him. He's a tough customer, and he's not hesitant to get right into somebody's face.

"Leonardo, although I've never had the pleasure of meeting you, your dad has told me all about you. I've also read a lot about you. You're one of the most accomplished people in the country, not to mention the smartest."

Uh oh. This guy is laying on the sauce for a reason, I think.

"Well, thank you, sir. I had a good upbringing."

"You're no longer the boy genius, but you're still a genius," he said. "Leonardo, I know all about your experience with the CIA, and how the idiots didn't follow your recommendations. Maybe it's because you were a kid at the time, but God knows we all saw what happened on 10/7 as a result of their ignoring your warnings. Your dad told me that the experience soured you on working with the government, and I can't say I blame you. But even though I can't blame you, I have an important request. Leonardo, of the many things I've read and heard about you, one is that you're a patriotic American who loves his country. Your heroic service in the Navy puts an exclamation point behind that."

"No argument there, Mr. Bixby."

"Please call me Tom. Leonardo, our country has a problem, a big one. Although you no longer have a security clearance, I'm going to be very straight with you because there isn't much time."

This guy does know how to communicate drama. I almost expected to hear a musical score behind him. But how does this involve me, I wondered. And what is the problem anyway? Eventually, Tom Bixby will tell me. Eventually.

"So, what is the problem, if I may ask, Mr. Bixby, I mean Tom?"

"October 7 of this year, Leonardo. That's six months from now. We believe that al Qaeda wants to repeat the horrors of 10/7, but this time make it even worse. We're not exactly sure what they're planning, but the Internet chatter leads a lot of our intelligence people to suspect they want to far exceed the events of 10/7."

"But Tom," I said, "I'm about to say something you already know, but the CIA has some really talented computer geeks. Haven't they made any inroads as to what may happen?"

"Yes, Leonardo, they have, but they need your amazing brain to help them understand what they're looking at. Leonardo, we believe we're faced with a gigantic terrorist plot. Because it's potentially a vast and complex operation, we believe we need the help of the best mind in the country, a mind that's used to dealing with vast and complex problems. Obviously, Leonardo, that would be you."

"I'm glad that my dad filled you in on my problems with the CIA, Tom. If the idiots had only listened to me, we could have avoided 10/7. What's going through my mind now is, 'Been there, done that.'"

"Big difference, Leonardo. You're no longer a little kid, but a grown man, with a background of honorable service as a naval officer. If you work with us on this threat, you will have executive authority, which means the ability to kick ass and fire people if necessary. Besides that, you will have my phone number, and I'm President Morton's chief of staff. Please help us, Leonardo. Our country needs you, my friend."

I woke up this morning thinking about the sea cruise I'm about to take with my beautiful new wife. Now this guy wants me to put my spook hat back on. But if I don't help them, who can?

"I can't turn you down, obviously. When you said that I'll have executive authority—and your phone number, that did it for me. I don't want some jerk asking me questions and ignoring my answers. My wife and I are going on our honeymoon tomorrow, a two-week European cruise. We'll board the *Queen Mary 2* in Manhattan. As my dad can tell you, my brain will begin to work on this problem."

"Don't worry, Tom. Leonardo will have sketched out the outline of an algorithm by the time the *Queen Mary* rounds Battery Park."

"Of course, Leonardo, we'll dust off your top-secret clearance, but please keep in mind that this is totally top secret, including your lovely new bride."

"Then I suggest, Tom, that you pull whatever strings you need to pull to get Janice top-secret clearance *immediately*. I don't keep anything from her. She helps me think. That's the way we operate. You want me? Janice is included. We're a package deal, a twofer. I'll be back in two weeks."

Chapter 45

Janice and I ate a light dinner in the kitchen. I thought of hiring a maid and a cook, like Ellen and Rick Bellamy did, but Janice hated the idea. Even though we can easily afford it, Janice felt it would hurt our privacy. I agreed with her. Besides, we both like to cook, and if we're pressed for time we can always go to a restaurant or order a catered meal.

We were already packed for our cruise, so I gave Janice a rundown on my meeting with Tom Bixby and my father. I told her everything that Bixby told me.

"Hey, Lee, I don't have any kind of security clearance. Are you sure it's okay to tell me this stuff?"

"Do you remember the wedding vows we took a couple of days ago? We are now one. I don't keep anything from you, and I made that clear to Bixby. You will have top-secret clearance in a few days, anyway."

"How is that possible?"

"I told Bixby to make it happen, as simple as that. A big difference from this assignment and the last one I worked on as a little kid is that I'll now have executive authority. As Bixby put it, I'll have the 'power to kick ass,' and to fire people. When we get back from the cruise, I'm expected to report to CIA headquarters. They have decent apartments there, not like this place, of course, but decent. No way will I order you around, but please say that you'll come with me. You'll have to take a leave of absence from your teaching. Since I'm chairman of the board at Champlin, I hereby give you permission to take leave. I haven't cleared it with CIA management yet, but they listen to me. They better listen to me."

"For a brainiac you're getting to be one tough guy. Of course, I'll come with you, honey. Actually, it sounds exciting."

Chapter 46

Our travel agent booked us into a Britannia Club Balcony stateroom, a huge suite on the upper deck of the *Queen Mary 2*. It had a fabulous view of the ocean, and plenty of room for us to play around, and we do love to play around. I didn't want to take away from the romance of a sea cruise, so I kept my conversation about our upcoming CIA project to a minimum.

"Hey, Lee. Is being on a cruise going to make you nostalgic for your Navy days?"

"This suite is a bit larger and more luxurious than my stateroom on the *Ford*. And I didn't get to room with a beautiful lady, just another guy. And I don't have to stand watch."

We had just checked in and unpacked our bags. The ship was due to depart in one hour at 5:30. I sat down to reread one of Janice's novels, always a great way to both relax and engage my brain. I was totally engrossed, not noticing that Janice had come back into the room. She walked over to me and stroked my face. She was stark naked.

"Hey, handsome, let's have a little pre-sailing fun."

Janice is never without ways to get my attention, and she had it, my undivided attention.

We made love, not even thinking about the ship leaving port. We had intended to be up on deck to watch the festivities as the ship departed, but, thanks to Janice, we had better things to do. We mutually climaxed as the ship's horn sounded. Cool.

We showered, dressed, and headed out onto deck, still feeling aglow from our pre-departure fun. The ship had just rounded Battery Park, with Frank Sinatra singing, "New York, New York," over the loudspeakers. We both love Sinatra, so it was a great way to start the cruise.

Our first day at sea saw a lot of rain. We decided to stay in our beautiful suite, which included its own hot tub. As Janice took off her robe and climbed into the tub next to me, an announcement came over the loud speaker.

"This is the captain speaking," came the announcement.

"I hope he realizes that he's interrupting something important," Janice said.

"This announcement is to advise you that this evening's show in the main theater has been cancelled. Please, join us for the show tomorrow. Sorry for the inconvenience."

"Now, where were we?" Janice said.

Janice and I had lived together for a few months before we married, and our relationship was far from celibate. But there was something about this cruise that was beyond special.

Sometimes we even missed meals because we were too busy in our suite.

The next day saw beautiful sunshine and moderate humidity. We steamed at a calm 15 knots. Janice and I walked hand in hand along the upper deck, drinking in the fresh air. We were due to arrive in Portsmouth, England, in four days.

"Hey, Lee, let's go to our room."

"But it's beautiful on deck today."

"It will still be beautiful later. Hey, we haven't had sex in four hours."

As I said, there's something special about this cruise.

Chapter 47

Janice and I pulled ourselves away from our suite and went to have lunch. People have to eat, no? We agreed that we didn't feel like standing in line at the buffet, so we opted to go to one of the main dining rooms where they have table service. We tend to eat less that way. If you don't watch yourself, you can gain 10 pounds on a sea cruise.

I had just taken a sip of coffee when I heard gunshots. I spit the coffee on the table. Then we heard more gunshots. My brain counted a total of 25 shots in all. What the hell was going on? We heard the sound of heavy footsteps running in the compartment over us. I found myself instinctively looking for a microphone, so I could announce general quarters and send everyone to their battle stations. Wouldn't have been a bad idea, as I would see shortly.

Two masked men ran into the dining room. They each carried an AK-47.

"Get under the table, honey," I whispered. "I think we're seeing a hijacking."

One of the men fired his rifle at the ceiling, causing a blizzard of falling plaster dust. Idiot.

From under the table we could see the feet of the other man running our way. Probably because his mask obscured his vision, the man tripped as he ran past our table. His rifle went flying in front of him. Janice, my sweet, gentle Janice, stood, swung her right leg back 90 degrees, and kicked the man's head as if she were going for a 50-yard field goal. The guy's unconscious face crashed into the deck. Janice crouched down and grabbed the man's weapon as she slid behind a column for protection from the other guy. She raised the rifle against her shoulder in a firing position, and flipped a switch, putting the AK-47 into fully automatic mode. She peeked out from behind the column and opened up on the other guy. He fell into the salad bar, dead.

"Somebody get that man's rifle," Janice yelled. Nobody moved.

Fortified by my wife's courage, I ran across the room and picked up the guy's gun.

"Come back here, Lee," she screamed. It seemed like a good idea, so I ran back to her position.

"I think we should stay here, honey, until we can figure out what's going on," Janice said.

The guy whose head she kicked began to stand. Janice fired three bursts at his torso and he collapsed to the floor. I just stared at her, not believing what I saw in the past two minutes.

"While things have calmed down a bit, hon," I said softly, "can you please tell me where this new ass-kicking commando Janice came from?"

"My dad was a Marine, and he wasn't satisfied until I could

handle at least 10 different weapons, and fire them accurately."

I stared at her, my suddenly amazing wife, who had just turned from a gentle, thoughtful, novelist into a machine-gun toting warrior.

"Everyone stay exactly where you are," came an announcement in a slightly Middle Eastern accent. "Do not move. This ship is now under command of the Islamic State. I am calling for a passenger named Leonardo Murphy to come to the bridge."

Janice reached over to the dead body next to our table and grabbed an extra magazine from the man's vest. She slammed it into her rifle and chambered a round.

"If those scumbags think they're going to harm a hair on your head, honey, they're going to have to come through me."

It was comforting to have Wonder Woman by my side.

"Hey, who's that?" Janice whispered.

A man in a chef's uniform came crawling toward us, cradling an M16 in his arms. He waved at us, indicating that he was friendly.

"I'm former Marine Sergeant Mike Parker. I'm the head of the ship's security detail, and it's my job to protect our passengers. Hey, nice shooting, lady. Who are you folks?"

"I'm Leonardo Murphy, and this is my wife, Janice Murphy. You can call her Rambo for short."

"Holy shit, Mr. Murphy. You're what this hijacking is all about. They want you, as you can surmise from the announcement you just heard."

"If anybody lays a finger on my husband, I'll blow his fucking head off," Janice advised.

"Okay, folks, listen up. This situation is far from hopeless. Twenty men and five women are in my security detail. We're all disguised like me, some as chefs, some as porters. Obviously, we were caught off guard. We count 15 hijackers, all armed with AK-47s. All that gunfire you heard a few minutes ago was simply their way of getting peoples' attention. Now, the three of us are going to crawl back into the kitchen where my surveillance monitor is located. I can see every compartment on the ship. All my people wear radio transmitters, so we can communicate—and make our attack plan. It's going to get nasty and noisy around here shortly, so you two keep your heads down. Mrs. Murphy, I'm amazed at how good you are with an AK-47. Were you in the Army or Marines?"

"My dad was a Marine."

"He taught his daughter well. But my job is to keep you safe, so please don't think about joining us in combat."

"Understood, as long as they don't step a goddam foot near my husband."

We crawled into the kitchen and stood. Sergeant Mike showed us his video surveillance unit. He wasn't kidding when he said he can monitor every space on the ship.

Mike held his microphone in front of his mouth.

"All units, Sergeant Mike here." He waited for responses.

"Can't the hijackers hear you, Mike?" I asked.

"All our transmitting devices are on a secure channel that nobody else can monitor."

One by one, Mike's security colleagues reported.

He carefully assigned any compartment containing a hijacker to one of his security people. Twelve of the fifteen hijackers were on the bridge, making Mike's battle plan a bit simpler. He assigned 19 people to attack the bridge.

"No arrests," Mike said into his microphone, "lethal force only."

As Mike had warned us, it got nasty and noisy. We watched the scene on the bridge from Mike's monitor as it became a war movie.

Nancy Boylan, the officer in charge of the bridge detail, looked at the security camera and flashed a thumbs up.

"Bridge is secure," Boylan said.

We watched as Mike's people attacked the three remaining hijackers. It was over—except for the cleanup.

Janice, smelling strongly of gunpowder, wrapped her arms around my neck.

"I can use a shower and then a soak in the hot tub," she said.

"Want company?"

"Of course, I want company. I want you where I can keep an eye on you. Gimme a kiss, baby."

Chapter 48

anice and I made the wildest love we ever enjoyed. Something about almost being killed stirs the passions. What's that old line? "Life's too short."

As we lay next to each other, exhausted, the phone rang. It was Buster calling from the CIA.

"Leonardo, it's Buster. I just got a full report on the hijacking. I know that guy Sergeant Mike Parker. You were in good hands, thank God. I'm coming to Portsmouth with a few other agents to meet you and Janice. Do not step foot off the ship in Portsmouth. Better yet, stay in your cabin. I'm sure newlyweds can figure out something to pass the time. We'll come get you. I guess you figured it out already, but your honeymoon is being cut short."

As the ship nudged into the dock in Portsmouth, we noticed the pier was covered with emergency vehicles. *The Queen Mary 2* had become a huge floating crime scene. As Buster insisted, we remained in our suite. Janice had placed her newly-acquired AK-47s next to the door.

Buster knocked on the door and identified himself. Four other CIA agents were with him.

"My friend Sergeant Mike told me all about Janice the warrior," Buster said. "God bless you, Janice. ISIS had big plans for Leonardo here, and presumably for you too. Your husband married a quite a woman. This is the third time somebody has tried to assassinate you, Leonardo, and it won't be the last. I have a recommendation, and I think Janice will agree with me. I know you aren't a violent man, even though you served in the armed forces, but I suggest that you carry a gun. I'm sure you learned to shoot in the Navy. I can put the paperwork through for you to get a concealed carry permit. You can practice at the shooting range at the CIA. You'll be safe at CIA headquarters, but I don't think you want to live out your life there. Once you've helped us with the project, I'm sure you two will want to return to New York. When that time comes, I'll assign two bodyguards for you. I understand that your house is large, so maybe you can put them up at your place. Janice, what do you think?"

"I agree with Buster, Lee. I think we both should carry guns. And we can easily house a couple of bodyguards at our place in New York."

"I've already concluded the same thing," I said. "Janice saved my life. She showed courage that was simply unbelievable. No way am I going to be in a position where I can't protect *her*."

Janice and I got into the limo that would take us to the airport. She leaned over and put her face next to mine.

"Too bad our cruise was cut short, Lee. I don't know about you, but I'll never forget it. Just because we won't be at sea, that doesn't mean we have to cut back on, well, you know."

"I completely agree," I said. "I hope the walls in our apartment at the CIA have sound insulation."

"What's wrong with making noise?"

"How about a kiss, Wonder Woman."

Chapter 49

**I** can't say I missed the CIA. Last time I was there, as a little kid, I did some outstanding computer work. The bozos didn't listen to me, however, and 10/7 was the result.

But those jerks are no longer there. I still have some good friends at the agency, certainly Buster and my computer pal, Jim Locklear, who stayed on as head of the IT Department. A couple of higher-ups gave me a lot of resistance when I said I wanted Janice to work with me. As I had told Bixby, the president's chief of staff, I wanted him to fast-track her for top-secret clearance. He did, so what's the problem? Bureaucracy. It seems that the new station chief didn't want to have a newly minted deputy agent—Janice—working on top secret stuff, even though she had the clearance. But Bixby had told me that I'd have executive decision-making power. So, I exercised that power and made it quite clear to the station chief that Janice is my partner.

I love working with Janice, I love to help her to outline a novel, and she loves to double-check my latest algorithm, not to mention critiquing my paintings. That brief cruise got our marriage off to a great start. But now I'm back in the spy business.

Our apartment at the CIA wasn't bad, although nothing compared to our Manhattan brownstone. It was roomy enough for the two of us at 1,300 square feet. The day after we moved in, I reported first thing in the morning to the shooting range to begin my new persona as a gun-toting spy. Janice came to the range too. She likes to keep up her proficiency with weapons. After she saved my life from those hijackers, I wasn't about to disagree with her. Naturally, before I begin something, I study. Last night, in a couple of hours, I read and memorized three books about guns. Even though I had small-arms training in the Navy, I felt like I knew the inner workings of any gun imaginable after my reading.

Janice thought my hip holster looked "cute," as she put it. I never thought of a gun as cute, but if she likes it, I'll learn to live with it. Janice and I agreed that we'd rather be doing something else, Janice with her writing and me with my new painting skills, not to mention my usual array of projects. But we knew this job was critical, so we put up with living at the CIA.

After a week on the shooting range, I felt good about my progress. I emptied the magazine of my pistol at a target 50 feet away. Every bullet hit the bullseye. Janice, no surprise, did the same.

Every day we met with Jim Locklear and reviewed the progress of my algorithm for finding terrorists. I began with the same program I invented nine years ago. Janice is smart as hell, and she quickly learned everything I taught her about computer systems design. She's not only smart, she has an amazing intuition. She could spot issues that even I overlooked.

Buster and Jim Locklear joined us. "Any early predictions for what may happen in October?" Buster asked.

"Janice thinks they may attack the nation's water supply," I said. "I may be good at handling tons of complex data, but Janice has an amazing way of picking the fly shit out of the pepper."

"My God," Buster said. "How did you conclude that the operation will involve the water supply?"

"Lee has really become quite fluent in Arabic, as you know Buster. I see you two yakking in Arabic all the time. Honey, why don't you fill these guys in on the details."

"If you recall my last program, I assigned values to words based on how many times they appear in communications."

"Did you see references to water?" Jim asked.

"No, not one. Just like ISIS did the last time, they use code words. One word we saw constantly was the Arabic word for 'juice.' I theorized that maybe they were talking about electricity. After Janice poured over my notes, she concluded, and I completely agree with her, that the Arabic word for juice means water in the ISIS code. Once she said that, it all started to piece together. They want to poison our juice, our water. I'll let Janice take it from here."

"Lee and I put together a list of the largest reservoirs in the country in terms of water capacity and came up with 122 of them. Their capacity is measured by a unit called an 'acre-foot.' It gives you the volume of water in a given location. It's simply an acre of water one-foot deep. Lake Mead, for example, the largest reservoir in the country, can store 32.4 million acre-feet of water."

"And what kind of contaminant do you think they intend to use?" Buster asked.

"Arsenic," I said, "the king of poisons. It occurs naturally in the environment. I didn't see any Arabic translation for the word, but the descriptions of the substance led me to conclude that it's definitely arsenic."

"And my big-brained husband is working on a formula that can show us how much arsenic it can take to lethally contaminate a given volume of water. We need your authorization to get us some arsenic so Lee can do tests."

"How the hell can we detect the stuff?" Buster asked. "My general knowledge tells me that arsenic is colorless, odorless, and tasteless."

"Forget detection," I said. "As a practical matter it can't be done. What I'm working on now is how we can spot large purchases of the stuff by people you wouldn't expect to be in the market for it, like farmers and pesticide manufacturers. We're working on the idea that somebody, presumably the Islamic State, is beginning to stockpile enormous amounts of arsenic. Delivery can be done by simply flying over a reservoir and dropping the necessary amount of poison. It can also be delivered by driving a truck into a reservoir. Fishing in a reservoir from a boat is allowed in some states, such as New York. That can further complicate the problem of identifying an arsenic delivery vehicle."

"Lee, you've only been at this for five days and look at what you and Janice have come up with."

"The name's Leonardo. Sorry Buster, but only Janice calls me anything other than Leonardo. I don't know why I care about this nonsense. I think it's a holdover from my childhood. But I prefer to be called Leonardo. Hey, I don't call you Gamal."

"You got it, Leonardo. I still have your sainthood application ready."

"Don't you have to die to become a saint?"

"I'm sure God will make an exception in your case."

Chapter 50

After our meeting with Buster and Jim Locklear, Janice and I went to the CIA gym for a workout. Janice insisted that we're spending too much time sitting in front of a computer, and we need to stay in shape. She was right, of course. Countless studies found that exercise improves mental work, and we sure as hell had a lot of mental work to do. And, of course, we don't confine our vigorous physical activity to the gym.

After our workout, we dined in the CIA cafeteria, where the food isn't bad at all. Pete Flanagan and Murry Bendel, our bodyguards, are polite about giving us space, but, on Buster's strict orders, they were never far from us. Our living quarters, of course, were bodyguard free.

We returned to our apartment at 6:30.

"Hey, let's make believe we're on a sea cruise," I said.

"What do you mean?"

"Let's go to bed and I'll show you what I mean."

"You never run out of wonderful ideas, do you, Lee?"

Murray's apartment was next to ours, and Pete's was on the other side. Janice and I tend to have noisy sex, so we always crank up the stereo when we make love. We play loud music a lot.

As we lay there after our cruise ship reverie, I lowered the volume on the music.

"Hey, honey, you seem to enjoy being a spy," I said.

"I gotta admit, Lee, that working with you on this stuff is fascinating. It gives me the opportunity to see your brain at work. But when I think that we're trying to prevent our country from being poisoned, I wouldn't call it fun. It scares the hell out of me to think about it. But my Lee is going to save us."

"I hope."

Although I didn't realize it, the next day my life would change.

Chapter 51

ee, are you happy with the progress of our water project? You've been kind of quiet about it lately."

"Water project? What water project?"

"Don't kid around, honey. We're getting together with Buster later and we've got to bring him up to date."

"Buster? What an interesting name. Is he a tough guy?"

"Lee, is everything okay? You seem to be, I don't know, kind of distant. I know you've got a lot on your mind, but your brain is big enough to handle anything. You seem stressed out. We should get more exercise, if you know what I mean?"

"No, what do you mean?"

"Wise guy. Hey, I'm going to run down to get us a couple of bagels from that new shop downstairs."

"Bay gull? Is that like a seagull?"

"You should be on *Saturday Night Live,* Mr. Comedian. I'll be right back."

—m—

"Sorry I took so long, honey, but I met Gloria Hirsch, that new lady in the IT department. She wanted to yack. I got us some lox and cream cheese, just what you like. Hey, Lee, cat got your tongue?"

"My name is Billy."

"Hey, don't kid around. We've got a lot to do today. Are you listening to me, Lee?"

"My name is Billy."

Janice walked over to the chair where Leonardo was sitting. She touched his hand.

"Hey, what are you doing?"

"I'm holding your hand, baby. What's the matter?"

"My name isn't baby. My name is Billy."

"Buster, you need to come to our apartment," Janice yelled into the phone.

"I'm about to go into a meeting, Janice. I'll be there in about an hour."

"Bag the meeting, Buster. Get up here now—*right fucking now!*"

Janice unlocked the door to let Buster in.

"Hi Janice. What's up?"

"Come in. I'll let reality speak for itself."

They walked to the den.

"Hi Leonardo. Nice pajamas if you don't mind me saying."

"My name is Billy."

Buster looked at Janice, who held out her hands, palms up, a look of confusion and fear on her face.

"Honey, I mean Billy, why don't you tell Buster what this thing is?" She put her hand on top of a desktop computer.

"A radio. I think."

"You look tired, honey. I don't think you got much sleep last night. Let's get you back to bed. Buster and I are going to have a cup of coffee."

They both led Leonardo into the bedroom. He stumbled twice, and didn't seem steady on his feet. They walked back to the den.

"Buster, what the hell is going on? Any idea?"

"I can't believe what I just saw, Janice. He reminded me of my grandfather. I hate to say it but Grandpa had Alzheimer's."

Janice put her face into her hands and sobbed.

"Easy, hon. I know how much Leonardo means to you. Don't worry. We'll figure this shit out."

Chapter 52

Buster, don't you remember those weird terrorist attacks a few years ago," Bill Carlini said. "What did we call it? Oh, yeah, *The Scent of Revenge*. A group of jihadis went around spraying a substance into people's faces giving them symptoms just like Alzheimer's."

Buster was sitting in Director Carlini's office, telling him about Leonardo's strange behavior.

"I'm going to call that psychiatrist from New York, the guy who's also a detective with the NYPD. Weinberg. Yeah, Dr. Benjamin Weinberg. He helped crack that *Scent of Revenge* case."

The next morning, Buster met Dr. (Bennie) Weinberg at the entrance to CIA headquarters. Bennie is 58 years old, about 5'9", handsome, but a bit overweight, which he compensates for by wearing expensively tailored designer suits. He's balding, but never tries to cover it with a comb-over. They went to Buster's office. Because Bennie had top-secret security clearance, Buster told him about the urgent matter that Leonardo was working on.

"This sounds like one cluster fuck, my friend," Bennie said. Even though he was a physician and Harvard Medical School graduate, Dr. Bennie's language is that of a New York City cop.

They went to the Murphys' apartment. Janice opened the door.

"Hey, Janice, you look like you haven't slept in a month," Buster said.

"I've been sleeping, if you can call it that, on the couch. Lee now thinks I'm his mother."

"Janice, can you tell us anything out of the ordinary that happened in the days before Leonardo started acting strange?" Bennie asked.

"I've been thinking of little else. Sorry, but nothing happened before Lee started acting this way. It just suddenly came out of the blue three days ago. He's not the same man I married, the most brilliant mind in the world. Shit, now he thinks a computer is a radio."

"Did anybody come to your apartment who you didn't recognize?"

"Well, yeah, the cleaning guy. Pete Flanagan, one of our bodyguards, said the man was okay."

"You said the 'cleaning guy.' Tell me more about him," Bennie said.

"He comes every two weeks. Or I should say, *a* cleaning guy comes every two weeks. The last one who showed up I had never seen before. Like I mentioned, Pete Flanagan said the guy was okay."

"Tell us exactly what he does—or did."

"He walked all around the apartment with a spray bottle of

cleaning fluid. Oh, right—I just remembered something. He accidentally sprayed the stuff into Lee's face. Lee didn't get angry or yell—you know what a gentleman Lee is. He just went to the sink and washed his face. I recall that the guy had an odd name. Oh, yeah, Adelberto, that's it."

Buster and Bennie stared at each other.

"I cannot fucking believe what I just heard, Buster. We thought we licked that goddam *Scent of Revenge* problem."

"Please tell me what you mean by *The Scent of Revenge*," Janice said as she shredded a napkin.

"A few years ago, we were hit by the weirdest, and cruelest, set of terror attacks we had ever seen. Jihadis were going around spraying a strange substance into the faces of young women. Then they expanded their victim targets. They put the stuff into the water system of a cruise ship, resulting in a ship full of people acting like zombies. The result was symptoms of Alzheimer's, just like you say is happening to your husband."

"Oh, dear God," Janice said with a sob. "Somebody has given my Lee Alzheimer's?"

"Hey, doll, don't worry. If this is what we think it is, it's curable with a drug. Before we try the drug, I'd like to examine your husband."

They went to Leonardo's bedroom.

"Lee, this is Doctor Weinberg, a friend of Buster's."

"My name is Billy."

"Hey, come into the bathroom, honey, I mean Billy." Leonardo had urinated all over himself and she wanted to clean him up.

He sat in his fresh pajamas and a bathrobe. Bennie asked him a dozen questions, just to confirm what seemed apparent.

"Dr. Ben, did you say it's treatable with a drug?"

"Hey, I'm taking a guess that the spray bottle contained the same substance that was used on those women and the cruise ship. If so, we're in luck. The drug is Tralforlalazine, an effective but seldom-used drug for treating the flu. The great thing about the drug is that it's been widely tested in clinical trials and approved by the FDA years ago. We already knew its side effects, which are rare and relatively mild—joint pain and headaches—both of which can be treated with over-the-counter medications like aspirin or ibuprofen. I'm writing out a prescription now. Buster, I suggest you take this to the CIA infirmary. I wouldn't be surprised if they carry the drug."

Buster almost ran out of the room. A few minutes later, Bennie's phone sounded.

"They carry the drug, Bennie. I'll be up in five minutes."

"Here, Leonardo, take this with that glass of water," Bennie said.

"My name is Billy."

"Sure thing, pal."

"My name is not pal. My name is Billy."

"You got it, Billy. Just take this tablet."

"He seems to be dozing off," Janice whispered.

"That's normal with Tralforlalazine."

Janice sat with her fingers intertwined, crying.

"Easy, doll. Buster told me how close you two are. I predict that your guy will come back to us in a few minutes."

Five minutes went by, then ten. Janice continued to cry. Bennie looked at his watch, then at Buster.

Leonardo shook his head, stretched his arms, and yawned.

"Hey, what the heck am I doing in my pajamas? And who is this gentleman?"

"Lee?"

"Hi, baby. What's going on?"

Janice wrapped her arms around my neck and kissed me.

They all started talking at once. A gaggle of voices explained what happened to me.

"While Leonardo was dozing I made a couple of phone calls," Buster said. "There is nobody employed by the CIA named Adelberto. He's the son of a bitch who sprayed a substance into your face, which resulted in the symptoms you just got over. Do you recall that, Leonardo?"

"Yes, I remember washing the stuff off in the sink. That's the last thing I remember. What was I like for the past three days?"

"You looked and acted like someone with a classic case of Alzheimer's disease," Bennie said.

"I just had your two bodyguards placed under arrest," Buster said. "I will be questioning them for quite a while. I've assigned two new guys as your bodyguards, who should be here in five minutes. I cannot believe that this shit happened right here at CIA headquarters. Leonardo, somebody is out to get you."

"And the bastard could have been after Janice too," I said. "I'm glad to hear you've locked up our bodyguards, the ones who didn't do much guarding."

"We'll be leaving you two," Buster said, as he and Bennie were walking out the door. "Let's get together tomorrow morning for a brief meeting, now that Leonardo is back with us."

"I need to take a shower," I said, after Buster and Bennie left.

"I could use a shower too?"

"Great idea. Follow me, and don't call me Billy."

"It's great to have you back, baby."

Chapter 53

The Murphys' bodyguards are still in custody, yes?" Bill Carlini asked Buster.

"Yes, they are. I questioned both for two hours yesterday, and I think their stories are bullshit. They didn't just miss seeing what was there, they were inside this goddam plot, way inside. They couldn't tell me anything about that spray cleaning guy, Adelberto. I mean, shit, how can bodyguards let a man into their subjects' apartment without knowing who he is? I gotta admit I'm nervous, Bill. How the hell can something like this happen at CIA headquarters of all places? If we aren't secure, what is? I've asked Leonardo and Janice to call or text me every half hour and they agreed. They're great people. The least I can do, the least we can do, is keep them safe. And now we've got another project on our plate. We all thought that *The Scent of Revenge* crap was over. Looks like it's back. At least we have a treatment drug available."

"How is the water project going, Buster?"

"Well, it was on hold for the three days that Leonardo was a space cadet, but, typical of him, he's back at it big time. Janice may not be as smart as Leonardo—hell, nobody is—but she's invaluable. As Leonardo puts it, she knows how to pick the fly shit out of the pepper. Those two are the most important assets the CIA has ever had. I told them that I'm going to assign two bodyguards to go back to New York with them when this is over. They own a huge building in Manhattan and agreed that they would put the bodyguards up at one of the apartments. I suppose you know that the Murphys are loaded. I mean they're filthy rich. No surprise that our genius friend figured out how to make good investments. The accounting department complained to me that the Murphys never cash their checks. I'm going to change it to direct deposit and make a note to remind them to transfer the money to their New York bank. Imagine never cashing your paycheck?"

"Just make sure that we can trust the bodyguards. I'm going to have internal affairs do an updated background test on every employee. We've got to know who we can trust. We thought we did, but we blew it with those two bastards."

Chapter 54

anice and I were having breakfast in the CIA cafeteria. Not exactly the Upper East Side of Manhattan, but it wasn't bad.

"I'll bet your brain has been working overtime since you came back to the world, honey."

"Something's bothering me. Do you think it's possible that the plotters may want to do a test run on one or two reservoirs, just before the main event?"

"I've been worried about that same thing, Lee. But don't you think they want to avoid showing their hand? I mean if they hit one or two reservoirs, the jurisdictions that control them will harden all the targets."

"The targets are pretty hard right now, but remember, given the right amount of arsenic and a simple method of delivery, the shit hits the fan real fast."

"Wolf Blitzer reporting for *CNN*, ladies and gentlemen. We've just gotten a disturbing report of an apparent poisoning of a reservoir in Kentucky. The Jackson reservoir is relatively small, and it serves a nearby village. Hundreds of people have been hospitalized and a few have died. The authorities have concluded that a large amount of arsenic was dropped into the water. Reports indicate that a small private plane was seen flying over the reservoir about an hour before the illnesses began. Intelligence authorities think this is a terrorist act. In a way that's obvious. Why would anyone other than a terrorist poison a water supply? FEMA has issued a warning to avoid drinking tap water. That's easy enough to say, but we use water for cooking and bathing, not just drinking. This situation is scary, to say the least. Please stay tuned to *CNN* for further updates on this disturbing story."

Chapter 55

"Leonardo, you've been sounding the alarm about the possibility of what just happened," Buster said.

"I won't say, 'I told you so,' because my big question is what you or anybody could have done to prevent it. If we can believe the news reports, the poison was dropped into the water by an airplane. I mean what the heck can we do, shoot down any plane that flies near a reservoir?"

"Just as Lee said last week before he spent a few days in la-la land," Janice said, "the way we're gonna beat this thing is to track purchases of arsenic and focus on large amounts bought."

"What about thefts?" Buster said. "Your thoughts on that, Leonardo?"

"Thefts are actually easier to track than purchases, because most of the time a theft is reported to the police. My algorithm tracks both and I'm beginning to see a pattern. Two or three more days should give us a much clearer picture, a picture that hopefully will include names. And I don't want us to go through what happened on 10/7, when we could have arrested the creeps before the attacks occurred. Once we have a few names, we can act. And if the CIA chooses to do nothing, Janice and I will arrest the bastards. We're both quite good with guns, now that I've been hitting the shooting range recently."

"Okay, wise guy. Don't go talking to me about you two becoming field agents, but your point is well taken. Once we have enough information, we'll act, not exercise our patience. I just got the latest information from Kentucky. My God, 580 people died, and that number is likely to go up as critically-ill people pass on. Don't worry, Leonardo, I'm ready to come out blasting as soon as your program gives us a believable list of names."

"I'm concerned about timing," Janice said. "Buster, I'm happy to hear you say that you want to act as soon as we have enough information. I've been watching Lee tweak the algorithm, and I think we'll soon have a critical mass of data."

Chapter 56

week went by, then two. Janice and I began to feel that we were approaching the Holy Grail, the critical mass of data. We were consumed with the fear that the terrorists would attack another reservoir any day, just as they did in Kentucky. How do you know when you've hit the right numbers? It's as much art as science, but, after consulting with Buster and Director Carlini, we agreed that one ton of arsenic, either purchased or stolen, combined with a minimum of five names on the watch list of people involved in the arsenic-related chatter, and we would be ready to act. I should say, Buster and the other field operatives would be ready to act. The names we get from my algorithm can provide the CIA with enough evidence to arrest them. Soon we'll have enough information to act.

One Thursday afternoon, Janice and I realized that we hit the numbers. Time to act. We were scheduled to meet the next morning with Buster and Carlini, and I didn't want to make a hurried announcement. I wanted to do a few more tweaks.

"I got your text last night that said you had a big announcement for us, Leonardo," Buster said. We were in Director Carlini's office. "So, don't keep us in suspense. What have you got?"

"Janice and I agree that we're ready to act, or I should say, you're ready to act. We have eight names that also appear on the CIA watch list, and twelve instances of large purchases or thefts of arsenic, all totaling just over one ton. All eight of the people discussed poisoning of reservoirs, although they didn't use those exact words. Gentlemen, you're good to go."

Buster slapped his hand on the table as he always does when he's excited about something.

"Leonardo, I have your sainthood application ready to go, with just one addition. It will be a joint application, including Janice. You two are the best thing that ever happened to the CIA, not to mention the country. It's time to roundup some scumbags. Great work."

Chapter 57

olf Blitzer for *CNN*, ladies and gentlemen. Reports are coming in about a major intelligence coup, as well as a large law enforcement effort. We are still reeling from that horrible story of the reservoir poisoning in Kentucky. A total of 605 people lost their lives from arsenic poisoning. CIA Director Bill Carlini has just announced eight arrests of suspected terrorists, as well as a seizure of over a ton of arsenic, the poison that was destined to be dropped into reservoirs across the country. I have with me on the line, Director Carlini.

"Mr. Director, please tell us about this incredibly important action."

"Thank you for having me on your show, Wolf. We've been working on this plot for months, and I'm happy to say we prevented what could have been one of the worst disasters in American history, rivaling the events of 9/11 and 10/7."

"Of course, you can't get into too much detail, but can you tell our viewers how this coup came about. Was it basic spy work with people on the ground gathering intelligence?"

"The breakthrough came from our IT department, where some imaginative computer experts enabled us to sift through tons of data, and I mean tons, and spot facts and trends."

"Those people sound like true American heroes, Mr. Director. Can you tell us who they are?"

"Don't even fucking *think* about it," Janice yelled, standing next to me as we watched the TV.

"Don't worry, hon. Carlini's cool."

"Wolf, you're absolutely correct at calling those folks true American heroes, but for obvious security reasons, they will remain unsung heroes."

"Wolf Blitzer signing off folks. Stay tuned to *CNN* for updates on this amazing story."

Chapter 58

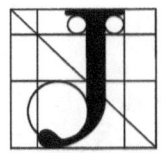anice and I returned to New York on a beautiful day in mid-May. Buster arranged for us to fly in the CIA Gulfstream G650—along with our new bodyguards, two guys who had gone through the most rigorous vetting process. The CIA people are still embarrassed by that *Scent of Revenge* crap that was sprayed into my face while my bodyguards stood by and did nothing.

It felt great to be back in our brownstone. Our CIA apartment was decent, but nothing like this place. The view from the living room is breathtaking. The weather was perfectly clear and sunny, and Central Park was proudly boasting its beautiful May foliage. I had arranged for a caretaker to look after the place while we were doing our spy bit at the CIA. He did a great job, and the house was spotless. Our new bodyguards, Jack Monahan and Sid Jordan, are nice guys, easy to get along with. They made clear to us that our privacy was a major concern, right after protecting us. They share a two-bedroom apartment on the floor below us.

"I think Buster is being overly cautious," I said to Jack Monahan. "I mean do we really need bodyguards?"

"Hey, Mr. Murphy..."

"Leonardo."

"Okay, Leonardo, let's look at some facts. There have been four attempts on your life, and at least three of them could have involved Janice as well. I don't know the details, of course, but Buster can't shut up talking about the work you did for us. He keeps referring to you as Saint Leonardo. Let me just say thank you for your service—to the CIA and the country. You and your wife are two great people, and Sid and I intend to keep you alive and well so that you can continue doing great things."

Easy guy to like. Buster, of course, took care of the details of getting Janice and me concealed-carry permits in New York. I gradually adjusted my mind to the idea of carrying a weapon all the time. I got a new shoulder holster, which Janice says makes me look like a TV detective. Janice carries her gun in a holster on her waist. Wonder Woman.

Janice and I were having a cocktail on our terrace overlooking the park, enjoying the view.

"I'm afraid my favorite novelist is getting rusty since our little trip to the CIA. Wanna share with me any ideas for your next book?"

"I think it will be a science fiction novel, based on our experiences with the CIA. It won't be called that in my book, of course, maybe something like GIA for Galactic Intelligence Agency. Of course, I'll need to keep our friends' identities secret, so I'll just make them friendly aliens. Buster's character will have a tentacle growing out of the back of his head."

I cracked up.

The phone rang. It was my mom.

"Great to have you two back home, Leonardo."

"Hey, Mom, why don't you and Dad join us here for dinner tonight. It's a beautiful evening."

She cupped the phone and yelled to my dad.

"We'll be at your lovely house in a half hour, honey."

Mom loves the house I bought. Money doesn't go far in Manhattan, but when you have as much as I do, it goes far enough.

My folks arrived in exactly one-half hour. They love to be punctual. I noticed that Mom was wearing a gun as usual.

I arranged for dinner to be catered by a neat little French restaurant down the street. We sat down to eat as the sun was about to set.

"Your dad and I worry about you two, Leonardo. It's not just because we're in law enforcement, but we are concerned about security, especially *your* security. I mean, my God, there have been four attempts on your life."

Mom can't help being a mom. I told them about our bodyguards downstairs and the fact that we now carry guns. I thought Mom would do a cartwheel.

"Dad and I had hoped to convince you to do just that."

"And I don't even have to pay them, not that I can't afford it. The CIA picks up the tab."

We had a great evening, soaking up my parent's attention. We told them all about Janice's novel writing, and my plans to start a publishing company. When I showed them the painting I gave to Janice I thought they'd faint. They had been on a European vacation when I gave it to Janice, and the only time they saw it was on *60 Minutes*. The view in person is much different than on a TV screen.

"Leonardo, this painting is breathtaking," Mom said. "I've never seen anything so beautiful. It looks exactly like the view from that pretty cabin we rented in the Catskills—exactly. It seems like that scene was firmly imprinted on your big brain."

We also spoke a bit about my latest invention idea, a house that cleans itself.

"Put me down for one of those," Mom said.

I felt relaxed, something that I hadn't felt in quite a while. Great parents, a wonderful wife, a mind full of ideas. But in the back of my brain, something was lurking. Something's cooking, but I didn't know what. Screw it, I thought. Enjoy the moment for a change.

Chapter 59

ow that we're done with our CIA spook adventure, we began to focus on Janice's writing career. She thinks I'm just being polite when I tell her how much I love her novels. But I mean it. I think she's gifted, and I wanted to start on my idea of setting up a publishing company, even if Janice is the only client. Having only one client has its advantages, like not having to put up with pain-in-the-ass phone calls from nervous literary agents.

We began our search for big-time editors. I'm always the first one to edit Janice's work after she completes a first draft. But I'm more like a line editor and proofreader. In a half-hour I can edit one of her manuscripts and make it completely free of spelling and grammatical errors. But I wanted an editor who can see things that I miss with the story and plot. I'm not a dummy when it comes to the big picture of developmental editing—hey, I created the Austen program—but it's not something I spent a lot of time training myself for. If we can't find the right editor, I'll just read some books about editing and I should be up to speed in a couple of days.

"So, tell me the idea behind your next novel?"

As is our rule, she never tells me the full story line, just the basic idea. She says, and I agree with her, that it's good for an editor—and I'm always her first editor—to read the book as a whole, not talking about it piecemeal.

"It's going to be a time travel novel. I've read a few recently and it looks like a fun genre to play with. The title will be, and of course I'm always open to your brilliant suggestions, *Friends in Time.* The basic idea is two passionate lovers who keep losing each other in different dimensions in time. It really interrupts their love life, because every time they achieve a mutual orgasm, one of them goes back or forward to a different era. As you may have noticed, the book will have a lot of humor in it."

"I love it. Maybe you should call it *Coming in Time.*"

Janice cracked up.

We were having a blast, as usual. Being involved in Janice's creative writing process is a joy. She was getting nervous about my plan for starting a big publishing company, so we put that idea on hold. We agreed that she should continue writing in our home. It's certainly big enough. To hire a big-time editor did not require that we open an office. These days, 99 percent of all publishing work is done electronically by email, like most everything else. Editors who we've worked with in the past can't wait to review Janice's manuscripts because they're completely free of errors (thanks to me) and the editor can get down to more creative tasks.

Whether it's doing spy stuff with the CIA or going over one of Janice's books, we love working together. I couldn't have been happier.

I'd soon learn that I had nothing to be happy about.

Chapter 60

The next day I took a cab down to Wall Street to meet with my investment guy, Jerry Blankfein. My bodyguard, Jack Monahan, was with me, of course. I really didn't need Jerry's advice, and I noticed that he often sought mine. But he does stay on top of things, which is great because I don't dwell on investing as much as I used to, preferring instead to work on one of my projects, or one of Janice's books. But I do like to make money, and Jerry frees me up to do other things.

I finished up with Jerry about 4 p.m., just in time to beat the rush hour heading uptown.

Right after Jack and I walked through the door of my house he pushed me against the wall, his finger on his lips asking for silence.

"Do you smell that?" he whispered.

"Yes," I said. "Holy shit, it smells like gunpowder."

"Stay here, Leonardo. I'm going to investigate. *Do not move.*"

I took his advice, although I did take out my Glock and chambered a round. My mind was occupied by one thought, one thought only. "Where's Janice?"

In five minutes, Jack walked swiftly but quietly back down the hallway, holding his gun in both hands, pointed up.

"Sid Jordan is dead. His body is outside your apartment. Come with me to open the door, but I want you outside in the hallway. Give me the key."

"I can open my own door."

"I don't want you doing something reckless. From the look on your face, I think you're considering just that."

Jack opened the door and stepped in gingerly. I held my Glock at my side. I waited for about four minutes, but it seemed more like four hours. Jack came to the door with his pistol in its holster. He looked relieved.

"I was afraid what I'd find in your apartment, Leonardo. After seeing Sid's dead body, I was scared shitless I'd find Janice, but she's not there. Of course, it's not entirely good news, my friend. It's obvious that Janice has been kidnapped."

Janice—kidnapped. I called my mother, who would oversee the Sid Jordan murder case anyway. I noticed that I was speaking in a monotone. My brain is accustomed to sorting through facts and coming up with conclusions, but it wasn't happening. I felt numb, brain dead. Janice is missing—and I had no idea where she was.

"Leonardo, relax, which I know is a ridiculous bullshit thing to say," Jack said. "The NYPD people are good with stuff like this. Hang in there, buddy. I know how much she means to you."

Three police cars pulled up to the front of the house. Because it's rush hour and we're on Fifth Avenue, one of Manhattan's busier streets, it took the cops about 20 minutes to arrive. As I expected, my mom was there. As chief homicide detective with the NYPD she always goes on a call when something big happens. Her son's bodyguard being murdered qualifies as something big, not to mention the kidnapping of her daughter-in-law.

Mom abandoned decorum and hugged me.

"Just take this one minute at a time, honey. A kidnapping always seems like the end of the world, but suddenly, clues begin to show up. As of now, we have no idea if this has something to do with the previous attempts on your life, or if it's just a kidnapping for ransom. I'm hoping it's the latter, because God knows you have enough money to pay a big ransom. We exchange the money for Janice, and then track the bastards down after she's safe."

Jack Monahan was standing next to us. He's not only a bodyguard, but a CIA agent. He knows a bit about criminal investigating.

"What I'm concerned about is timing," Jack said. "I believe this happened between two and six hours ago because Sid's body is already showing signs of *rigor mortis*. I was just in the apartment with your colleagues and we listened to the answering machine. No messages. No ransom demands. As a detective you know more about this than I do, Mrs. Murphy, but I would have expected a ransom demand long before now."

"Our phone is unlisted," I said, "but I'm not sure what that means."

"Anybody who planned this action knows how to get an unlisted phone number," Mom said, "and they probably figured out how to get your cell phone number too, Leonardo. I agree with Jack here. It doesn't look like a ransom kidnapping."

"Great," I said. "It looks like terrorism. I wish to hell I never agreed to work for the CIA. I put a target on Janice's back as well as mine."

"Hey, honey," Mom said, "remember, we need to take this minute by minute. I'm going upstairs now to supervise the crime scene investigation. You stay here, or maybe in Jack's apartment. I don't want you to go through anything worse than what you're going through already."

"No, Mom, if it's okay with you I'd like to be there. You need a lot of brains working on this, and I think I've got a pretty good one. Besides, your people probably will want to ask me questions as they're going through the evidence."

I managed to walk into our apartment without falling unconscious. I was scared as hell about what I may see, but I wanted to be there.

"Here's a gun," a cop yelled from the den. We walked into the room as he was putting the gun—Janice's Glock—into an evidence bag. "It was in the drawer of that table over there, next to the computer. It hasn't been fired."

I walked over to Janice's computer and sat down. It was still running.

"Hey, pal, if you're going to help us put these on," one of the detectives said.

He handed me a pair of latex gloves. Oh, right. Crime scene.

"Did I hear you say this is your wife's gun?"

"Yes, we both have concealed carry permits, but we seldom wear our guns when we're in the apartment. Hey, we have bodyguards."

I immediately apologized to Jack Monahan for my wiseass comment. Poor Sid was killed trying to do his job.

The document Janice was working on was still on the screen. I looked at today's word count. Like me, Janice keeps a careful word count when she's working on a book.

"This file was saved at 11:15 a.m., over six hours ago," I said. "She had only written 500 words, which tells me that she intended to do a lot more writing. Janice has a rule for herself to write a minimum of 2,000 words a day when she's working on a first draft.

"*Oh my God, look at this*," I shouted.

Mom walked over. "What are you seeing, Leonardo?"

"Janice had the sound recording software turned on. She does that so she can make a quick voice note as she's typing. Besides recording sounds, the software also transcribes the spoken words into a separate text document. The software shows the time of day next to the words."

I moved the cursor to 11 a.m., a few minutes earlier than the time I think she stopped typing.

We heard the words spoken as well as seeing them on the screen. "Do not move, Mrs. Murphy, or I will shoot you," said the voice in a heavy Middle Eastern accent.

"Who the fuck are you?" we heard Janice say. Wonder Woman. Please keep your mouth shut, baby, I thought to myself.

"Mrs. Murphy, you will accompany us to a car waiting in the parking area at the rear of the building. We are taking you to Englewood, New Jersey. You will be safe as long as you don't say a word. If you try to resist or escape you will be killed."

"I can't believe it," Mom shouted. "This is a gift. Obviously this idiot didn't know he was being recorded. He even gave us a location."

Jack Monahan was already on the secure phone with Buster, who was en route to New York in the Gulfstream.

"Jack, can you tell us anything about Englewood?" Mom asked.

"Yes. We've been tracking the activities at a house in Englewood that al Qaeda has been using as a safe house. They don't know that it's not safe—*for them*. Buster just told me that one of our agents, who occupies a house next door to the safe house, reported a car with two males and one blond female, pulling into the driveway at 11:45 this morning. We have the place under tight surveillance as you might imagine. We're not out of the woods yet, but at least we know where to focus our efforts."

I felt like a thousand pounds was just lifted off my shoulders. She's still in the custody of terrorists, but at least we know where she is.

"Now what?" I asked.

"Leonardo, my friend, the CIA is very good at hostage situations," Jack said. "I mean we're *really good* at this shit. Hang in there buddy. We're a lot closer now than we were 40 minutes ago. Buster will meet us at our location along with a few other agents."

Mom wrapped her arms around my neck. "I was negative as hell when I first got here, honey. I've worked with these CIA guys before. As Jack said, they're *really good* at this shit. I just spoke to Dad. He's going to meet you at the house in Englewood. Obviously, this involves the Joint Terrorism Task Force. He told me that Rick Bellamy, Janice's brother-in-law, will be there too. As Secretary of Homeland Security, this involves him as well. Don't worry, Leo, your lovely wife will be in your arms shortly."

"That's Leonardo, Mom," I corrected her. I figured a little lame humor couldn't hurt.

"Mom? I take it you mean 'mother dearest.'"

Touché.

Mom, or Mother Dearest, has a way of calming me down.

Chapter 61

My dad was waiting for us at the CIA house in Englewood, New Jersey. Buster had just arrived. My God, I thought, Buster moves at the speed of light. I learned that he took the CIA Gulfstream from Langley to an airport nearby. Our surveillance house was getting a bit crowded. The house next door was 3211 Sycamore Avenue, the al Qaeda "safe house," the house where Janice is being held hostage. I felt strange knowing that I was no more than 300 feet from her. It was more than strange, it was frightening. I'd been through some scary shit in the Navy, but nothing like this. Rick Bellamy, Buster, and my dad stood in a corner, talking. I walked over to them. I felt like I had soggy armpits down to my knees. The most aggravating thing about our situation was that there was nothing we could do.

"I know you've probably heard this a thousand times in the past couple of hours, but hang in there, Leonardo," my dad said. "Janice will be okay. Between the CIA and the FBI, we know quite a bit about situations like this."

Dad was looking over my shoulder at the house next door as we spoke.

"Oh my God, am I seeing things?" he said.

I turned around and looked out the window. Janice, *my Janice,* was calmly walking across the lawn to the house we were in. I ran out the door, almost tripping over my feet. Janice saw me and ran toward me. Later we would have a laugh about how the scene must have looked, like something out of an old war movie, where the long-separated lovers run toward each other on a beach. We hugged for what seemed like an hour. Everybody filed out of the house onto the lawn.

"Everybody back into the house," Buster shouted at the top of his lungs. "I want that place secured," he said to the security detail.

"Don't worry about it, Buster" Janice said, "the place is secure."

"Who secured it?" Buster yelled.

"I did. Sorry but you folks will need to clean up the mess I made in there," Janice said, pointing a thumb over her shoulder.

"Mess?" Buster said.

"Yeah, I shot four people. Their bodies are all on the first floor."

Wonder Woman.

Buster, who was the senior agent in charge of the operation, asked Janice to come into the kitchen so he could take her statement for the record. I sat next to her.

"I always thought these terrorist types were slick and smart," Janice said. "How's this for smart? While I was sitting at the kitchen table eating some slop they served me, one of the idiots put his AK-47 on the table in front of me—right in front of me. I was hungry—I hadn't had anything to eat in hours. But when I saw the rifle, I figured I would eat later. So, I grabbed the gun and opened fire. All four of the jerks were right nearby, none of them holding a weapon. I guess I was lucky to be kidnapped by idiots."

"What were their demands?" Buster said.

"Only one demand. They wanted to capture this handsome man next to me, and they wanted me to call Lee and arrange for a meeting place. I stalled as much as I could, telling them that Lee's phone apparently was not working. The jerks believed me. Hey, guys, if we're done here, I'd like to go home and take a shower to get the smell of gunpowder off me."

I figured that a welcome home party was called for, so I invited Janice's folks, my parents, the Bellamys, Buster, and Jack Monahan. Everybody gathered in the den and sipped drinks. I went into our bedroom to check on Janice. We hadn't been alone the whole time. She came out of the shower wrapped in a towel. We hugged. Then we kissed. Then we hugged some more.

How can she be so calm? I wondered. Not for long. She buried her face in my chest and sobbed.

After Janice and I collected our wits, we joined our guests in the den. My mom gave Janice a hug, and said, "Don't hold anything in, honey. Talk your brains out. Believe me, I've been involved in a lot of tense and scary situations. Your head will feel much better if you talk out all your fear and upset. Don't keep it bottled up." As always, Mom is way cool.

Janice took Mom's advice, and talked all about her frightening adventure, crying occasionally.

"Thank God you left the recording software on in your computer," I said. "If it wasn't for that we'd still be wondering where you were."

So, Janice's kidnapping had a happy ending, thank God. Janice and I had targets on our backs, and it's futile to think that we can erase them. The only thing we can do is be vigilant. But isn't that what bodyguards are for?

As the last people left the party, Janice and I walked into the bedroom, looking forward to an evening of passion. We both fell fast asleep as soon as our heads hit the pillow.

The day after the party I addressed myself to the task of returning our lives to normal. But then I realized that we don't live normal lives, so why bother.

But at least I can try to make our lives safer.

Chapter 62

henever I have a problem, I always do the same thing. I study, research, and think. The issue in front of me, the sole issue, was security. Buster suggested that we place video monitors in every room in our house. But how could we be present with the monitors sending out alarms to our bodyguards whenever we make the slightest move? So, I invented a "client specific" security monitor. I wrote a program that enables the monitoring devices to distinguish between Janice and me and a stranger. I can program the devices on the fly, so that bells don't go off when our cleaning lady or one of our bodyguards comes by.

I also invented a state-of-the-art (well, I *think* it's state-of-the-art) alarm device that Janice and I carry at all times. With a press of the button, it either sends out an alarm to a predetermined location or records a message or both. It's sort of like that help button for elderly people who have fallen and can't get up. But our alarms and recordings are sent to four locations that I specified—My mom's cell phone and my dad's, and the cell phones of each of our bodyguards. If somebody wants to kidnap one of us, they will have to deal with the chief NYPD homicide detective, the head of the Joint Terrorism Task Force, and a couple of trained CIA agents. The hand-held alarms were Mom's idea, and Dad readily agreed.

Janice and I concluded, based on Mom's suggestion, that we

should always wear our guns, even when we're in our apartment. Not when we're sleeping, of course. I would notify our bodyguards when we were turning in, and one of them would sit in a chair outside our apartment, often reading one of Janice's novels.

We also bought a watch dog, a big goofy Golden Retriever we named Spook. Whenever somebody came into the apartment who Spook didn't recognize, her way of protecting us was always the same. She would pee on the floor and lick the person's hand, never once barking.

It's a good thing our house is large, because we spent a lot of time there. A 3,700 square-foot rooftop garden included a running track around the perimeter. Spook loved to hang out on our roof. We installed a 10 by 20-foot outdoor synthetic grass carpet for Spook. I invented a small device that I call a *Spookalator*. It sends out high frequency sound waves. When pointed at a pile of Spook poop, the sound waves render the crap into a small mound of inert dust. The *Spookalator* also dries out and deodorizes the carpet. My attorney has been negotiating with General Electric, which is interested in buying the patent rights to the Spookalator. Their most recent offer was $5 billion. We also have the same setup on our 15 by 30-foot terrace two floors below. On both the roof and the terrace we installed a ten-foot high sheet of bullet-proof glass. This was Buster's idea, and my folks cheered it. "Nothing will ruin your day like a bullet in your head," Buster the wiseass said. In one of the large bedrooms on the second floor we installed a gym with 15 exercise machines. Since we spend so much time here, we figured we should stay in shape. Our bodyguards, Jack Monahan and Murry Bendel, are free to use the gym whenever they want, and they often do.

Janice wants to get back to her writing, and I want to continue painting as well as work on my usual array of projects. We thought we were out of the spy and law enforcement business, but it wasn't working out that way, as Janice's kidnapping reminded us.

I keep trying to live in the present and not worry about something that hasn't happened yet. I try, but it isn't working. It isn't comfortable knowing that you and your wife are being hunted. What's next, I wondered.

Chapter 63

anice and I admitted something crazy to each other. We enjoyed being spies. Although it made our lives a bit scary with the recent attempts on our lives, not to mention Janice's kidnapping, we missed spook work. Janice actually loved it. We got to work together and solve complicated problems. Janice continued to write and I continued to paint and work on my other projects but we sort of missed the excitement of being spies.

We had no intention of going back to the CIA, but we both realized that, if the government needed us to solve a serious national security problem, we couldn't decline—for ethical reasons. If we can keep the country safe, why not? And who better than us?

This morning, Mom called and said she needed to see us, so we invited her for lunch. I had no idea what it was about, but she sounded uncharacteristically upset. In her line of work, Mom isn't easily ruffled, causing me to wonder what was going on. As soon as Spook heard the doorbell, she ran to the door to serve as our protector. She peed on the floor and licked Mom's hands—both of them.

Mom kissed Janice and me and said, "Can we sit down at the kitchen table, Leonardo?"

"Hey Mom, you called me Leonardo."

"I believe you mean 'Mother Dearest.'"

She may be upset about something, but her sense of humor is firmly intact.

"I've been a homicide detective since before you were born, honey, but I'm up against something that has me totally stumped. You've read about the rash of murders recently that has everybody thinking that a serial killer is behind them, I'm sure."

"Yes, Mom," Janice said. "I read about that in the *Times* this morning. Lee and I talked about it. My God, it almost seems like a plot for a horror movie. I mean 20 bodies so far. I've never heard of anything so creepy."

"We're trying to keep it from the press so as not to start a panic," Mom said, "but we think the body count is more like 50. Fifty dead bodies—in one month. The earmarks are all the same, as you would expect from a serial killer. But what has me going nuts is the timing of the murders. They've occurred all over New York City in all five boroughs, but the real shocker is that a bunch of the killings were done around the same time. We could be looking at serial killers, plural, not just a serial killer. Leonardo, Janice, I'm asking for your help. You two are amazing at figuring out stuff that looks impossible to understand. We've got to stop this killing. Most of the murders were of young couples. Most were married, but a few were just dating or engaged. Because you two are a young couple, I beg you not to go anywhere without your guns and your bodyguards. Better yet, just hang out in your beautiful house. This case reminds me of that horrible human being, Son of Sam, a few years ago, to use the words human being broadly."

"Do you suspect any particular group?" I asked.

"It almost seems like MS-13, but as we all know, thanks to you, Leonardo, that gang has been virtually wiped out. And the victims don't fit the typical MS-13 target profile. As chief detective, I'm embarrassed to say this, but we don't have a lead or a clue. The bodies just keep piling up."

"Do you think this may involve terrorism? The numbers seem to point that way," I said as I took a pitcher of ice water out of the refrigerator.

"Nothing's off the table, honey. Because the signs possibly indicate terror, this matter has your dad's attention, too, as head of the Joint Terrorism Task Force. This case needs Leonardo Murphy's brain as well as that of his able wife. You don't need to come to police headquarters. You can patch into our mainframe from here by our secure Intranet server. Leonardo, we're looking for patterns, which is something you're astonishing at spotting. Thus far, the only pattern we've identified is young couples. In one case a woman was killed and her husband was murdered four days later. The poor kids had just gotten married only a month ago. Why in the world would anybody or any group target young couples? I just don't know."

"Mom, I mean Mother Dearest, can you get me the files on each of the murders? Obviously, I need to look at similarities, including the possibility that the murdered couples may have known one another."

"I've got detectives fanned out all over the city trying to get information exactly like that. Leonardo, Janice, I need you guys to connect the dots. Will you help me?"

"Are you kidding? Of course, we'll help you," I said. "I'm already starting to put together the algorithm in my head."

Spook, her tail wagging furiously, put a toy bone onto Mom's lap.

"Spook is trying to cheer you up, Mom. Don't worry, Janice and I will find this bastard—or bastards."

"Here are the login credentials for you to access our database."

"Does this case have a name, Mom?"

"We're calling it *Special K* as in cereal, which sounds like *serial*. Witty, no?"

"No."

"I don't think so either. It was the police commissioner's idea, not mine. You'll have to live with it. I do."

Chapter 64

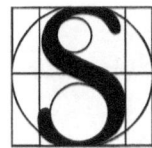o, hon, it looks like we're back in the spook business."

When I said the word spook, Spook nuzzled my crotch and wagged her tail.

"I hate to see your mom so upset, Lee. You can see the stress on the poor woman's face. She's famous as a sharp detective, but she's up against something even she can't figure out. I think it's great you agreed to help her."

"Hey, *we* agreed to help her. Remember, we're a twofer."

"A twofer? I love that. Hey, let's login and start to work. If this case wasn't so horrifying, I'd say it will be fun."

"Working with my Wonder Woman is always fun, babe. Before we start to look at the case details and the numbers, let's first do a little brainstorming,"

"*Brain*storm with Leonardo Murphy? I hope I don't get blown away by the storm."

"Okay, let's pose the first big question," I said. "Why would somebody target young couples?"

"Sounds to me like it could be a case of insane envy," Janice said. "Somebody hates to see young happy couples because the killer is not happy. Maybe it's a person who was jilted, and wants to take it out on people that the killer wishes he could be?"

"Crystal-clear thinking, hon, but if you're right we have a problem. Wanna guess what it is?"

"Yeah, where the hell do we find a database of people who were jilted?" Janice said.

"Divorce records?"

"Lee, something tells me the killer is not divorced. Even if he was divorced, I don't see where that would lead us. If you're correct that he's envious of young couples, wouldn't that mean he hates them because that's who he wanted to be—a young man in love with a young woman? And we're not sure it's a man."

I walked across the kitchen to get us some coffee. Spook ran to help me. As I brought the pot to the coffee table, Spook jumped onto the couch and sat on Janice's lap, licking her face as she did so.

"I think we can start with a working hypothesis that it's a man—or a very strong woman. Those murders were horribly violent. And from what I've read, serial killers are seldom women. I recall reading that only about one in six serial killers is female. Oh, hey, didn't my mom say the victims were couples, not just married couples?"

"You're right, Lee. So how do we figure out how somebody targets a couple of happy people?"

"Simplicity itself. The killer could just sit in an outdoor cafe and look at young couples holding hands or kissing."

"Yeah, Lee, but if you see a couple kissing or holding hands, that doesn't get you into a friggin database does it? I mean the bastard doesn't jump up and yell, 'Hey, I'm going to kill you two.' We'll know a lot more when we start to research the victims, but identifying the killer is starting to look pretty hard."

"Sure, it's hard. That's why the police don't have any leads yet, and that's why my mom came to us. If it was easy they would have locked the guy up by now."

"Another thing, Lee. We keep talking about the killer in the singular. You agreed with your mom that this case has some earmarks of terrorism and that there may be more than one killer involved."

"Right now, nothing's off the table. We need to pour through the data we already have and keep working it as the cops find more evidence. We can't lock ourselves into a theory. That Son of Sam slimeball, David Berkowitz, was nailed after basic and careful police work. He killed six people and wounded seven. The scumbag or scumbags that we're after killed 50, according to my mom. Let's log in to the police computer."

Chapter 65

've found that to solve a mystery it takes more than brains; it takes attitude. By that I don't mean something as simple as a positive attitude; it takes an aggressive attitude. Janice and I didn't crack those CIA cases just by sifting through data, we solved them because we refused to give in to preconceived notions. When Janice came up with the reservoir-poisoning theory at first I thought she was way off track. Turns out, she was right on target. She refused to let herself be boxed in by flaky assumptions. I learned a hell of a lot from her when we worked that case. Wonder Woman.

Within two days, we had a lot of data on the victims, the 50 dead people. We both agreed we would adopt a Zen-like "blank mind," and follow the evidence where it took us, rather than let any predetermined notions take over. Of course, we formed hypotheses and theories, but we refused to let a theory rule our minds. Follow the evidence. Don't necessarily trust the evidence but follow it until it leads somewhere—or nowhere.

The patterns were starting to form. Of the 50 victims so far, not one person was over the age of 35, and 60 percent of them—30 people—were under 25. Janice wanted to turn herself loose on the soft evidence, stuff that doesn't jump off the page. She poured over photographs of the victims, photos taken before they were killed, of course. She wanted to see if the victims could be described as "good-looking." What is good-looking?

Some people are obviously "good looking," Janice for example. Every few hours we would huddle and look at the photographs, which Janice ranked as "very good-looking" to "somewhat good-looking." Of course, it's a subjective hunt, but we were amazed that the two of us agreed on almost every photograph.

"This is one hell of a lot of good-looking people," Janice said.

"So, let's play with a hypothesis," I said. "If the killer or killers targets good-looking people, could that mean that he's not good-looking? Getting back to your original theory that the killer is consumed with envy, this could be an interesting direction. But how? Do we advise the cops to be on the lookout for homely-looking people, people who may be envious of good-looking people? That nice guy who's a waiter in the diner around the corner could be a primary suspect because he's homely as hell."

We agreed that we had come upon an important data point—but we also agreed to put it on the shelf, because we just couldn't see where it was leading us. But it was a data point, an important one.

Chapter 66

Wolf Blitzer for *CNN*, ladies and gentlemen. I have a horrific story to share with you today. The death toll in New York City's wave of apparent serial murders has climbed dramatically. The NYPD had been telling us for weeks that the number of dead victims was around 20. We have now learned, from a reliable inside source, that the real number is 50. That was until yesterday. It has now climbed by 10, in just one night, to 60. The police don't know, or I should say they haven't told us, whether they suspect one killer is responsible or if it's a group. Perhaps understandably, the police department is not being free with information, because the killer or killers are very much on the loose. We *have* been told some details of the similarities in the murders. I warn you, that the information I'm about to tell you can be quite graphic. You may want to ask your children to leave the room. Although I'm going to go over facts that the Police Commissioner James Borden himself has given us, *CNN* has chosen to not disclose some of the details, because, frankly, they're just too gruesome for television. Here are the facts:

- Of the 60 people murdered, not one was over the age 35, and 60 percent of the victims were under age 25.

- The murders were all committed with knives or guns or a combination of the two.

- A disturbing detail in all the murders, and here is where it becomes quite horrible, all— that's every one of the victims— had their eyes gouged out,

- All the murders occurred in the five boroughs of New York City.

- A development which leads the police to suspect that more than one killer may be responsible is the fact that at least 10 of the murders occurred closely in time, indicating that more than one person could be involved.

"A lot more details are buried in the information we've received, but *CNN* management has decided that some of the details are simply too grisly to discuss on the air. Needless to say, we will be tracking this shocking turn of events closely.

"In other news…"

Chapter 67

atching the morning news can be a tough way to start your day, especially if you're working on a case that makes gruesome headlines daily. Janice and I couldn't believe the reports of the 10 new serial-killer murders last night. Although we had a hard time believing what we heard, after spending an hour on the phone with Mom this morning we knew the reports were accurate.

Our project has become personal. My mother entrusted the research of this case to Janice and me, and no way in hell will we let her down. We saw it as our personal responsibility to save the next couple. Last night's 10 murders put an exclamation point to our work.

"Lee, honey, I feel like throwing up. Your mom has put a lot of faith in you."

"And you."

"Yeah fine, but I see my job as an assistant to the brain of Leonardo Murphy. Honey, we need to put everything else on hold. I want to put a stop to this horrible shit, and to find the animal or animals and hand the evidence to your mother. Everything's got to stop until we handle this."

"Even making love?"

"Hey, Lee, do you feel particularly amorous right now?"

"I have to admit I don't, babe. I thought I'd never say that, but this case has me thinking of nothing else. Let's get this done. One of the many benefits to stopping this mayhem is that we'll get back to sex."

Janice didn't find my crack particularly witty. Neither did I.

"When we find them, Lee, I'd like to personally shoot those bastards."

"Hey, calm down, Wonder Woman."

"After the work we did last night, I feel like we're making progress," Janice said, "but not enough progress. Hon, let's get to work."

We often go out for breakfast—with our bodyguards, of course. But we both agreed we didn't want to waste a minute of time. We placed our computers side by side, so we could ask and get feedback from each other as we worked through the data. Jack Monahan, one of our bodyguards, brought us some bagels.

"So, what do we know this morning that we didn't know last night, Lee?"

"Well, for one thing, last night's murders occurred over six hours. Two people were killed in each of the five boroughs, about an hour apart, according to forensic reports. So last night's killings could have been committed by one man. Each of the murders saw the same disgusting earmarks as all the others—The victims' eyes were gouged out."

"I've lost my appetite," Janice said as she pushed her bagel away.

"Fred Dempsey said he wants to come over and talk about some new stuff he's uncovered."

Detective Lieutenant Fred Dempsey is my mom's right-hand man. He's a sharp-as-hell detective, and he's also a nice guy. It would have been easier if Janice and I worked on our stuff at police headquarters, but Mom wouldn't hear of it. I guess she's right. The killer or killers targets young couples. And Janice and I are a young couple.

"Hi, Leonardo, Hi, Janice," Fred said as he tried to keep Spook from jumping all over him. Spook seems to have a special fondness for cops, whether they're in uniform or not. "Something new showed up in last night's killings. We didn't dare leak it to the press. The killer is stamping the victims with this."

He showed us a photo of what looked like a tattoo, a circle about three inches in diameter filled with markings that looked like something from Italy in the Middle Ages. I recognized that because I'm fluent in Italian, although not Middle-Ages Italian. It was a crisp, clear photo. I took it to my scanner and uploaded it to Google Images so I could plug it into my program to search across the Internet for similar designs. I also planned to research the image to see if we could glean any meaning from it. I began my search as we spoke. I'm good at multi-tasking, so talking to Fred and Janice while searching didn't slow me down a bit.

"Leonardo, at the risk of repeating what I've said many times, you are fucking amazing. Pardon my *copspeak*, Janice. I've been here, what, five minutes, and already you're chasing down similar images."

"Bingo," I said. "Look at this on the Wikimedia website. I count a dozen shots of that same image. Hey, look at this one. It includes an explanation of what the image means. I was right, it is from the Middle Ages."

"So, what does it mean?" Janice said.

"It's a symbol for murder."

"I just want to caution you, Leonardo," Fred said. "From the serial murder cases I've worked on, and I've handled a lot of them, killers often leave a calling card, such as that image. But it doesn't necessarily mean that it symbolizes anything. It could just mean that the killer finds the image pleasing."

"But it *could* symbolize something," I said. "We already know that it's a symbol for murder. I'm going to put that image into my algorithm and automatically search the Internet for repeated occurrences. By Internet, I'm including public emails, Facebook, Twitter, and all the other social media sites. I doubt the guy would be stupid enough to post the image on social media, but maybe we'll get lucky."

"Fred," Janice said, "have you guys been thinking much about the killer's mental status? I mean do you think maybe he's a psychopath or one of a group of psychopaths?"

"That's been a working hypothesis, Janice, but you may be surprised to know that serial killers aren't all nuts. Some of the big names in serial killer history have definitely been diagnosed as psychopaths, such as John Wayne Gacy or Ted Bundy, but some of them were not insane, just unbelievably cruel. Hey, listen, since we're talking about psychology, I think I know a guy who should be working with us on this case. He's a psychiatrist as well as a New York City detective."

"Bennie Weinberg?" we both asked.

"Yeah, do you know the guy?"

Janice and I told Fred all about my days as a space cadet when I was inflicted with that *Scent of Revenge* stuff.

"Bennie is brilliant, no doubt about it. I mean he's not as brilliant as Leonardo here, but who is? I know he's working on another matter now, but I'm going to ask your mom to reassign Bennie to this case. I think she'll agree in a heartbeat, and I'm sure the commissioner will too."

Chapter 68

om works fast, no doubt about it. And if it's something involving the *Special K* case, she moves at the speed of light. I still think that's a stupid name for a criminal investigation, but the commissioner likes the name, so we all have to live with it, as Mom reminds me.

Bennie showed up at our house promptly at 8 a.m. As we had told him, we'd enjoy a breakfast of bagels and lox from a great deli a couple of blocks away.

Bennie wore khaki slacks and an expensive Brooks Brothers jacket. He masks his slight portliness with expensive clothes. After I got to know him I kidded him about being a psychiatrist who worries about personal vanity.

"Janice, Leonardo, great to see you two again. Or is it Billy?"

"Wise guy. Pass the lox please. I'm surprised to see you here so soon."

"Your mom is a persuasive lady. I was working on depositions for a big extortion case, but she got the commissioner to allow me to jump on this *Special K* matter. Dumb name, if you ask me, but nobody did."

Bennie is popularly known as Bennie-the-Bullshit-Detector. He sits in on a lot of depositions and trials to advise the prosecuting attorney if a witness is lying. He's developed a method of spotting lies based on a given number of physical movements and facial gestures. Prosecutors love him. They say it's like having a witness hooked up to a lie detector.

"Leonardo, you're probably a thousand years ahead of me, so let me start with a general question for both of you, and here it is. What do you want to know from me about this serial killer or killers?"

"Janice and I assume, as I guess most people do, that the killer is insane, a psychopath. Are we working with a level-headed assumption? Give us your professional opinion as a psychiatrist and as a detective."

"This may surprise the two of you, but a lot of serial killers are not clinically insane, just evil and cruel. Son of Sam is a case in point. Berkowitz originally told investigators that he was responding to the voice of a demon in his head, a dog named Harvey which belonged to his neighbor, Sam. Most shrinks, myself included, upon hearing that information diagnosed him as a psychopath. But it subsequently came out that his story was a bullshit hoax, and he admitted as much. He was found competent to stand trial. When I first read about the case, I assumed he was a psychopath, but I was wrong."

"Bennie," Janice said, "could you please explain what exactly a psychopath is and how it differs from a sociopath? Lee and I have been researching both terms and there seems to be a lot of disagreement among mental health professionals as to what the words mean."

"There's a lot of overlap between those two diagnoses, but there are definitely distinctions between the two, and those distinctions aren't too subtle. Start with the word, 'conscience.' Sociopaths and psychopaths both suffer from a lack of conscience, or I should say it's their victims who do the suffering. If you or I did something bad to another person, our conscience would suffer. The reason our conscience kicks in is because we're normal people—and we have a conscience. If somebody falls in front of us we offer to help him up. If we hear a baby suddenly cry, we want to know what the problem is. Society couldn't exist without this thing called conscience. It's sort of like a deal we all make with one another. If I hurt you, my conscience will bother me and I'll feel bad, which means I probably wouldn't have hurt you in the first place."

"What are the major differences between a sociopath and a psychopath, Bennie?" I asked.

"Let me start with psychopaths," Bennie said. "Some of the most dangerous motherfuckers on the planet are psychopaths." Bennie's New York cop mouth was on full display. "They're dangerous because they tend to be highly intelligent, are fond of planning their evil work, and couldn't give a rat's ass how much they hurt their victims. They can be articulate, loquacious, and charming, even holding leadership positions. Most researchers think that psychopathy is a genetic malformation of the mind. Yeah, they're born that way, or at least with a tendency to be that way. They may even be happy, if you define the word happy broadly.

"Sociopaths, on the other hand, also exhibit a lack of conscience, but not in all cases. They tend to be unhappy losers. Most mental health researchers think that a sociopath gets fucked up because of nurture, not nature. For example, an unhappy childhood from being constantly bullied, a pattern the sociopath imagines is constantly repeating as he goes through life. If you or I get treated badly by a surly waitress, we shrug it off and maybe leave a smaller tip. But the sociopath would see it as a personal attack on him."

"Do you have a hypothesis that you're working on, Bennie?" Janice asked.

"Yes, my money is on the word psychopath. I see a hell of a lot of planning going on in these killings. These murders aren't spontaneous acts of anger or any other emotion. They seem to be carefully planned out. I mean shit, in the 10 killings that happened the other night, they all occurred in New York City, and in each of the five boroughs. The killer knew what he was doing, including figuring out how to get from one location to another to do his stuff. But what really nails it for me and makes me think the killer is a psychopath are the things he does to his victims. Dear Lord, eye gouging? If all he wanted to do was kill the victims, why take out their eyes? I spoke to the medical examiner yesterday. He's found evidence that, at least in four of the murders, the killer gouged out the victim's eyes while the person was still alive. Yeah, this scumbag is a psychopath, one of the worst I've ever seen. A lot of research, not to mention some confessions of serial killers, indicates that some psychopaths get sexual pleasure from his acts. Can you imagine getting sexual gratification from gouging somebody's eyes out?"

"Bennie, what about that stamp that the killer has been putting on the bodies, the one that Lee says comes from the Middle Ages? Lee's research tells him it's an old Italian symbol for murder."

"A lot of psychopaths want to have fun. It's his way of flipping a middle finger at the cops. The history of serial killings has seen this plenty of times. TV writers use a killer's 'calling card' to make the show more exiting. But, besides exciting television, it *is* a reflection of the truth. The good news is this: Leaving a calling card is risky and reckless. Eventually, we'll see a clue. The bastard doesn't know that he's up against the brain of Leonardo here. My bet is that Leonardo will come out on top like he always does. It takes one hell of a psychopath to outwit Leonardo Murphy."

My cell phone rang.

"It's my mom," I announced, "I'm putting her on speaker."

"Turn on the TV," Mom said.

"Shepard Smith for *Fox News* ladies and gentlemen. Here in New York, it's 3 p.m., and there's been another two murders bearing the earmarks of the vicious serial killer who's been haunting our city for the past few weeks. The killings took place within the past two hours in none other than Battery Park, a place that's seldom without a lot of people wandering around. The victims, as in the other killings, were a young couple in their twenties. As in all the other incidents, both victims had their eyes gouged out. Every one of the now 62 killings have been shocking to say the least. What's extra horrible about this one is that it was committed in a public park in broad daylight. I'll be bringing you updates on this senseless slaughter as we learn more."

"Your thoughts, Bennie?" I said.

"I've seen this before. This guy is extremely bright. He's taunting us and trying to show us that he's beyond our reach. Broad daylight? In a heavily-trafficked park? What's next, a video?"

Chapter 69

Sometimes I need to be alone. Sometimes I need to think, just think, without talking to other people. Sometimes I revert to being the loner I was at Harvard. Janice and Bennie are smart as hell, and great to work with, especially my Wonder Woman. Bennie stayed until 10 last night, and then Janice and I continued the conversation for another hour.

But I needed to talk—to my algorithm. I didn't need any more brainstorming or the give and take of ideas. I woke up at 3 a.m. and decided to go into cyber-think.

By now I had a huge amount of data, the way I like it. The more data, the more comparisons I can make, and the more I see data points cross each other. I felt the same feeling when I'm on the verge of any breakthrough. I felt like the time when I launched my first satellite into space. I knew I had enough data, and the satellite in orbit proved it.

I know who the killers are, yes, the killers, plural. I know where they live, and I know their names. I think I even know when they may strike next.

Nobody lives in a complete vacuum, cut off entirely from society, even slimeballs who torture and kill innocent people. Inevitably, a killer makes his presence known.

But even though I went into solitary mode, I know enough to realize when I need to bring other people into the world my brain came up with.

Janice walked into the den at 5 a.m. with coffee for us.

"This self-imposed celibacy sucks, Lee. I really want to wrap up this friggin case so we can go back to making love."

"If I'm correct about what I've found in the past two hours, hon, you and I will soon be having the hottest sex imaginable."

"You have my undivided attention, baby. What have you found?"

"I'm calling my mom. I want her and Bennie to come here and meet with us. I think I've broken this case."

"Honey, it's just after five. You're not going to call them now, are you?"

"When I give them a hint at what I'm thinking about, I think they'll be here in less than an hour."

Mom showed up at 6:15, and Bennie was right behind her. They each live less than a mile from our house. Mom brought with her Adele Maxwell, a sharp assistant district attorney in charge of the *Special K* prosecution. Adele is about 35, tall, almost lanky, with a pretty face except she looked tired as hell. Well, that's probably because Mom woke her at five.

"When you called me, I was in the middle of a fucking nightmare, Leonardo," Bennie said. "The nightmare was about our psychopath killer friend. So, tell me my nightmare's over."

"You mean our psychopathic killer *friends*, Bennie. Yes, that's plural."

"Leo, honey," Mom said, "I think I speak for the three of us when I say we're listening."

I didn't even correct Mom for calling me Leo.

"Let me summarize and then I'll drill down into the details. There are four of them, all males, and all former members of MS-13. I poured over my MS-13 algorithm and I've discovered that the symbol we found on the recent bodies was popular as one of the MS-13 tattoos. Here's the most important part—I have their names and addresses."

I handed Mom a piece of paper with the information.

Mom, Janice, Bennie, and Adele just stared without saying a word. Then Mom spoke.

"Leo, I mean Leonardo (as always, Mom is way cool), did these men chat on the Internet. I mean how did you find this information?"

"Although it's illegal, I hacked into all of their computers. Easy to do, actually. I remembered my MS-13 algorithm, and the unspeakable cruelty of the gang members. So, I followed my hunch and looked at that data. As they did before, they communicated in the code language Caliche. Sometimes they wrote in Spanish without trying to disguise their words. Idiots. How about this little missive from the leader a few days ago:

'Hey dudes, how 'bout we do some eyeball pickin tonight?' That was the afternoon before the 10 killings in one night. In one exchange between *all four of them,* they even mentioned the names of two of the victims. If I may make a recommendation, Mom, I suggest you round up these killers as soon as possible."

Mom was already on her cell phone barking orders to people at police headquarters.

She looked at us. She was so excited she was almost smiling.

"Adele, obviously we need to get subpoenas and warrants as soon as possible," Mom said. "You can use the information Leonardo just gave us for the probable cause affidavit. There's always a judge on duty in the early morning for a situation exactly like this."

"I won't mention in the application that Leonardo got the information by hacking private computers," Adele said. "Hey, he got a lot of information from data he already had. Besides, no way in hell would any judge question how we got information on four vicious murderers. May I use your computer to type out the applications, Leonardo?"

"Of course," I said. Wow, this lady works fast.

"Chief Detective Murphy here will have the police commissioner himself call the judge when we find out who's handling arrest warrant applications this morning," Adele said.

After Adele filled in the application online, she called her assistant at his apartment.

"I don't care how early it is, Jim. Get your ass to the courthouse and get in front of the after-hours judge."

"Okay, I'm going to make this a SWAT Team operation," Mom said. She moves as fast as Adele the prosecutor.

SWAT stands for Special Weapons and Tactics. All major police departments as well as the FBI field offices around the country have SWAT teams at their disposal. SWAT teams are used for high risk situations, such as hostage incidents, or a case like this where the arrest targets are vicious killers. A SWAT team mission is more of a military type action than a typical law enforcement operation. Mom arranged for four *Enhanced* SWAT teams, with a force of 40 officers and heavy-duty weapons, including MP5/10 machine guns and M4 carbines. She didn't want to take any chances of blowing this case.

"Leonardo, because of you this case is almost closed. We haven't made the arrests yet, but my SWAT Team people are great. Keep your phone handy. We'll be calling you throughout the day."

"No problem, Mom," Janice said. "Lee and I will be kind of busy, but this case takes precedence over everything else." Janice was sitting next to me at our kitchen table. She squeezed my knee when she said that we'd be "kind of busy."

"Kind of busy?" Mom asked.

"Yeah, organizing files and stuff like that."

"Stuff like that?" I asked. I was having fun playing with Janice's head.

"Yeah, *all sorts of stuff,*" she said, as she looked into my eyes and squeezed my knee again.

Chapter 70

Project *Special K* was closed within two days as a police investigation along with its stupid name. It was now in the hands of the prosecutors. All four men were arrested two nights ago by the SWAT teams. One man tried to escape by climbing onto a fire escape. He was shot and killed. Because New York law no longer allows the death penalty, the prosecution will seek life imprisonment without the possibility of parole.

Janice and I returned to normal, whatever normal is, after we were free from the pressure of the *Special K* investigation.

"So, we're no longer spooks," I said. Spook came running when she heard the word and put one of her toys in my lap.

"Hey, Lee, since we don't have any crimes to solve or terror attacks to prevent, what are you going to turn your big brain loose on now?"

"I've been thinking of a few things, and I need your opinion. Here they are:

- A new recipe for jelly beans. Maybe a jelly bean that tastes like pastrami.

- A milk-free milkshake.

- Alcohol-free Scotch.

- A self-shaking Martini.

- A device that translates dog barks into English.

"Any recommendations?"

"Yes, Lee honey, I do have a recommendation," she said, laughing.

"So, what is it?"

"Don't be an asshole."

CHARACTERS *LEONARDO MURPHY*

Bellamy, Ellen – Talk show host
Bellamy, Rick – Secretary of Homeland Security, Ellen's Husband
Ben – Owner of a dojo, a martial arts training school
Bendel, Murry – CIA bodyguard
Bixby, Thomas – President Morton's Chief of Staff
Blankfein, Jerry – Financial advisor
Borden, Frank – NYPD Police Commissioner
Buster – CIA Agent
Carlini, William – CIA Director
Dempsey. Fred – NYPD Detective Lieutenant
Donovan, Mark – CIA station chief
Fenton, Harry – Admiral – Leonardo's superior officer
Fenton, Meg – Lieutenant – Admiral Harry's Wife
Flanagan, Pete – CIA Bodyguard
Guevara, Angel – Assistant to MS-13 Leader Eduardo Lopez
Jackson, Gladys – FBI Agent in charge of a safe-house
Jordan, Sid – CIA Bodyguard in New York
Locklear, Jim – Head of the CIA IT department
Lopez, Eduardo – MS-13 Gang Leader in New York
Maxwell, Adele – Assistant District Attorney
Monahan, Jack – CIA Bodyguard in New York
Munson, Jimmy – A bully
Murphy, Ezekiel– Leonardo's great grandfather
Murphy, Jack – FBI Agent and Leonardo's father
Murphy, Leonardo – Itinerant genius
Murphy, Rebecca – Homicide Detective and Leonardo's mother
Parker, Mike – Former marine. Queen Mary II security head
Randazzo, Frank – Leonardo's attorney
Reynolds, Bob – Janice's father
Reynolds, Janice – Ellen Bellamy's sister
Reynolds, Melinda – Janice's mother
Rimland, Nat – President of Champlin College
Thurgood, Sam – Leonardo's accountant
Weinberg, Bennie – Detective Psychiatrist

A PERSONAL REQUEST

I hope you enjoyed reading *Leonardo Murphy* as much as I enjoyed writing it. Leonardo and Janice are now two of my favorite characters, and will both play a major role in my next book, *A Sea of Fear,* to be published in the winter of 2019. Please consider leaving a brief review of *Leonardo Murphy* on amazon. com or your favorite book site.

THE BOOKS OF RUSS MORAN

All books are available on Amazon.com, and also as ebooks on The Kindle or a Kindle app on your smartphone or iPad.

The Gray Ship – Book One of The Time Magnet Series
http://amzn.to/16GPumH

"This provocative, intensely powerful novel is a must-read for sci-fi fans and Civil War aficionados, though mainstream fiction readers will find it heart-rending and inspiring as well. A rare read that's not only wildly entertaining, but also profoundly moving." – Kirkus Reviews

The Thanksgiving Gang – Book Two of The Time Magnet Series http://amzn.to/1NzBs7N

"I had never read a book before written in an efficient, minimalistic prose. Instead of writing what most readers want to read, he gives voice to life-like characters, with their flaws and prejudices. They are not infallible superheroes. It's always nice to find a new voice in fiction and to enjoy creativity at its best." – C. Ludewig.

"Breakneck pacing and virtually nonstop action." – Kirkus Reviews

A Time of Fear – Book Three of The Time Magnet Series
http://amzn.to/1zdjaG9

"His story is fascinating, and adds even more depth to this already cavernously deep novel. Amazingly unique, chilling and well written, Moran weaves a future that is both desperate and hopeful. Blending modern fears with science fiction

results in a tale that will keep you reading long into the night."
Five stars!" – Heather

The Skies of Time – **Book Four of The Time Magnet Series** http://amzn.to/1CCC3jg

In *The Skies of Time*, you will recognize the two main characters, Ashley Patterson, now an admiral, and her husband, Jack Thurber. They met and fell in love in *The Gray Ship*, and now they're in for the adventure of their lives in *The Skies of Time*. Ashley and Jack have been such prominent characters in all four books of *The Time Magnet Series* that I feel like they're old friends. You will also recognize some of the other characters. But if I told you who they are, it would ruin the fun.

"I'm big fan of this series and this one may be the best. I hope there is another book to this series since it keeps getting better. There are a few questions I have about certain events that makes the next one even more suspenseful. These are great books to binge read one after the other." — Time Travel Fan

The Shadows of Terror – **Book One of the Patterns Series** http://amzn.to/1IDQzJS

A novel that explodes off the front page of your newspaper.

Terrorism has a new face, a face that's obscured in the shadows. The radical forces of destruction have learned to make themselves invisible to the West, and preventing a terrorist attack has become almost impossible.

A new war has begun, World War III.

Rick Bellamy, an FBI agent who specializes in counterterrorism, is engaged in his own war, a war with no end.

Bellamy's wife, Ellen, a prominent architect, discovers that she's in the middle of the greatest terror plot to date.

To defeat the enemy, Bellamy first has to uncover the clues, to shine a light on the shadows. He has to find patterns – before it's too late.

"Move over James Patterson and Mary Higgins Clark. There's a new guy in town. Russ Moran's new book – *The Shadows of Terror.*" – Frank O.

The Scent of Revenge - Book Two in the Patterns Series
http://amzn.to/1UvDRmw

The world is at war with the forces of terror. FBI Agent Rick Bellamy and his wife, Ellen, find themselves in the middle of a sinister terrorist plot.

Someone is attacking young prominent women, inflicting a horrible disease.

Nobody knows its origin, nobody knows how to stop it, nobody knows how to cure it.

Rick Bellamy and a team of scientists want to go on the offense. But how?

Will the lives of the women be changed forever? When will the attacks stop?

"Heart pounding, can't put down thriller that will force you to look at terrorism in different light. Life in America will never be the same." – Cold Coffee Cafe

Sideswiped - Book One in the Matt Blake series of legal thrillers http://amzn.to/1MkxX35

Trial lawyer Matt Blake took on a perfect case.

It involved a sideswipe collision in which his client's husband, an investigative reporter, was killed. The evidence of negligence was overwhelming. Eyewitnesses testified that defendant was talking on his cell phone when he hit the other car.

But was it negligence? Was it an accident?

Or was it murder?

Matt uncovers evidence that the act may have been intentional. Somebody wanted the man silenced. Somebody wanted the man dead.

Somebody had a lot to hide.

The signs started to point to the highest levels of government.

An open-and-shut personal injury case suddenly became a vast conspiracy of terror.

"This book hooks you in from the first line. *Sideswiped* draws you into the world of Matt Blake and you become emotionally attached to him and his journey. The story itself is so well-written and moves quickly there is never a dull moment." – Sarah Elle

"Moran demonstrates the depth of his writing talent by developing a new genre with *Sideswiped*, a legal thriller. Branching out from his previous novels dealing with time travel, Moran goes in a whole new direction with Book One in the Matt Blake series. He creates a wild but totally believable story of modern day intrigue and suspense. Moran also deftly weaves into this book some of my favorite characters from his prior novels. I am looking forward to starting Book #2 - *The*

Reformers." – Frank from Lynbrook on August 16, 2016

The Reformers - Book Two of the Matt Blake series of legal thrillers, is the sequel to *Sideswiped*.
http://amzn.to/2m8uMdu

The forces of radical Islam are on the run.

Their leadership has been decimated, their ranks thinned, their power disappearing by the week.

Their recruiting efforts have been cut off, the radical websites shut down, and the attraction of jihad is losing its appeal among the young.

With targeted assassinations, military strikes, as well as the loss of oil fields and gold mines, radical Islam is fast losing power.

But who is responsible?

It isn't the United States Government. It's a new force the world has never seen before.

Lawyer Matt Blake and his wife Diana find themselves in the middle of the most gigantic plot the world has ever seen, a conspiracy that's only begun to grow.

"I've been a fan of the author, Russell Moran, since reading *Sideswiped* a few months ago, so I admittedly went into this book with quite high expectations. That being said, I had no idea that *"The Reformers"* was going to play out in the way that it does and I can see myself giving this book a re-read in the future. In fact, I am even more impressed by the storyline of this read than the last and it has left me excited to see more." – Lucidity

The Keepers of Time – **Book Five of the Time Magnet Series** http://amzn.to/2wjVSTt

Admiral Ashley Patterson and her husband Jack have done it again. They've traveled through time, 200 years into the future—aboard a nuclear aircraft carrier, Ashley's flagship.

They discover a new world, a strange new world—a post-nuclear war world—one that is both a beacon of hope, and a cry of despair.

They meet a group of people who call themselves The Keepers of Time, an organization dedicated to preserving history and culture amid the horrors of a dystopian future.

The world around them has harkened back to a primitive and savage past, one that includes human sacrifice.

Ashley knows they must have to get back to the present to warn the government of the unspeakable horrors that await.

But finding the way back to the present is their greatest challenge, an almost insurmountable one.

"A wild time travel yarn that starts fast and doesn't slow down until the end."

A Reunion in Time
http://amzn.to/2tneIsg

What if a 37-year-old adult travels back 20 years in time and finds himself in high school, followed by his 36-year-old wife? They're now teenagers, 17 and 16.

Adults in teenage bodies, they struggle to convince the people from their past that they are real, not apparitions. With the benefit of hindsight, they know the history of the past 20 years, and it isn't pretty.

Rick and Ellen are married, and now have to adjust to married life as teenagers in 2001. Rick is a senior FBI official and Ellen is a famous architect.

But everybody sees them as kids. Nobody believes that they're married, and nobody believes their stories—until Rick and Ellen predict 9/11.

How do they find their way back to the year they came from? How do they warn the authorities of the cataclysm that will occur in the future? The answer is to find the time portal—the wormhole—that brought them to 2001. But the site has changed. It's no longer the place where they crossed the wormhole. Will they live out the balance of their lives beginning as teenagers?

"We've all wish we could go back to earlier times with the mind we have now. This Russell Moran book takes you there and it is a fun creative romp well worth reading. *A Reunion in Time* is highly recommend!" – Kindle Customer.

The President is Missing – Book Three of the Matt Blake series http://amzn.to/2t9v7wu

While he was addressing the nation from a submerged nuclear submarine, President Blake's message is suddenly cut off. Anyone listening heard an explosion. The explosion was followed by floating debris five minutes later.

First Lady Dee Blake has doubts, which she shares with naval high command and the new president. She thinks the explosion and the debris were a ruse to make people think the sub was destroyed, and her husband with it.

Could the sub have been hijacked and the president kidnapped?

But who would commit such an act? What is its purpose?

Was it Russia, China, Iran, or a shadowy group of freelance terrorists?

The new president appoints Dee as his Chief of Staff, with explicit instructions to find the missing submarine—and President Matt Blake.

Her life, and the life of the nation, suddenly take a horrifying turn.

Robot Depot
http://amzn.to/2zXW7C2

Mike Bateman is a visionary businessman, the creator and CEO of the fabulously successful chain of stores, Robot Depot, a company dedicated to selling robots and Artificial Intelligence machines for a variety of uses.

The company is a darling of Wall Street and is the most popular destination for consumers and businesses looking for labor saving devices.

But the company caught the eye of ISIS, the terrorist Islamic State. They discover a great way to deliver bombs – using the products of Robot Depot to kill people.

Robot Depot changed from being a popular company to an object of fear because of the tampered products it sells. The terrorists use the company for "terror spectaculars," including the destruction of a skyscraper, a drone attack on Yankee Stadium, and the bombing of a children's sailing regatta.

Mike Bateman and the FBI are in a race to stop his products from becoming weapons, a race to stop the wanton killings. His wife and partner, Jenny, discovers the true meaning of terror one horrible summer day.

A Climate of Doubt
https://amzn.to/2OSwcHR

A book that looks at the horrors of climate change, and how it became a weapon of terrorism. Published in May of 2018. It's Book Four of the Matt Blake Series. Matt and Dee Blake take on their biggest challenge to date, along with our old friends, Rick and Ellen Bellamy.

"A compelling read about a complex topic. Mr. Moran does a masterful job of crafting an action-packed, suspenseful read about the devastating consequences of climate manipulation." – Colorado Avid Reader

The Maltese Incident – A Novel of Time Travel (Book One of the Harry and Meg Series)
https://amzn.to/2RclZCT

The prequel to *The Violent Sea*. The story of a cruise ship, captained by Harry Fenton, that travels 100 million years to the past. Published in June 2018.

"AN AMAZING READ!! THE MALTESE INCIDENT is an absolute FANTASTIC MUST READ ! ! RUSSELL MORAN is my new All time Favorite Author now, I am following him to be able to catch all of his great works." – MaryKate5.

The Violent Sea – A Novel of Time Travel (Book Two of the Harry and Meg Series)
https://amzn.to/2QeJoDw

The sequel to *The Maltese Incident*. Admiral Harry and Lieutenant Meg Fenton ("America's Twofer") travel through time and change the history of World War II at the Battle of Leyte Gulf. Harry and Meg come out of retirement and return to the Navy. Published in October, 2018.

"Russell Moran has crafted a great continuation from *The Maltese Incident* his character development has continued from the first book thru out this book and possibly beyond. His writing is so detail oriented you will find yourself believing that time travel is not only real but possible." – Amazon reviewer. Published in October, 2018.

ABOUT THE AUTHOR

In addition to the 15 novels discussed above, I also published five nonfiction books: *Justice in America: How it Works—How it Fails; The APT Principle: The Business Plan That You Carry in Your Head; Boating Basics: The Boattalk Book of Boating Tips; If You're Injured: A Consumer Guide to Personal Injury Law; How to Create More Time.* My latest nonfiction book *The Novel - A Writer's Guide - Discover the Joy of Writing Fiction,* was published in October 2018.

I'm a lawyer and a veteran of the United States Navy. I live on Long Island, New York, with my wife and editor, Lynda, and our two dogs, Sammy the Shih Tzu and Maggie the Golden Retriever.